# The Protectors: Once Upon a Catastrophe

D1706296

# The Protectors: Once Upon a Catastrophe

The characters, places, and events that take place in this book are fictional. Any similarities to real people, living or dead, is coincidental and not intended by the author

Copyright © 2012 Rebecca Bourque

All Rights Reserved.
No part of this publication may be reproduced, distributed or transmitted in any form or by any means, or stored in a database or retrieval system, without prior written consent of the author.

ID:  13024006

Lulu
http://www.lulu.com/

# The Protectors: Once Upon a Catastrophe

# The Protectors: Once Upon a Catastrophe

# The Protectors: Once Upon a Catastrophe

# The
# Protectors

Part 1: Once Upon A Catastrophe

# The Protectors: Once Upon a Catastrophe

*For my parents,*

*my Protectors.*

# The Protectors: Once Upon a Catastrophe

# Prologue

People say, "if at first you don't succeed, try, try again", and, sure, that's great advice, but what if there is no "try again" option?

You know *those* people?

"When you fall off", they would say with a plastered smile, "just get right back up on that horse."

To which I would reply morbidly: "What if you're trampled by hooves and you die?" A remark like that would usually leave most stumped and stumbling over words.

Then, shocked and sometimes offended at my blunt disregard for proper conversational etiquette, they would leave, wondering why they attempted to speak with me in the first place.

Honestly, though, there are no second chances in the real world, believe me, I would know.

For me and my family, every choice ends up being life or death. Everything from battle strategies down to what socks we put in the morning. Oh yeah.

We didn't choose this lifestyle though. That's for sure.

And we definitely did not choose to be thrown out into the world, up against monsters and monstrous men, singled out and hunted down because of who we are- at least, it didn't start out that way.

Be it fate, or God, we were born at a deliberate point in time, with certain chromosomes, into a specific society, just in time to be involved in a very important life, and then caught in the middle of a very life-changing event. And so, because of all this, we were given a very precise purpose.

Now every single day, we choose to defend the destiny we were given- and to fight against any and all forces that would attempt to destroy us. It's not easy, but I suppose you could say we're stubborn.

You can consider this your cordial invitation to join our adventure; we sure could use the help.

You're about to make a choice, and although I'm pretty sure it's not a life or death matter for you- you can just walk away- some of us are not so fortunate.

# The Protectors: Once Upon a Catastrophe

# Chapter 1

I woke in my bed as pearly-orange morning light shone through my now-open windows.

Another day, another sunrise blooming over the ocean.

I got out of bed, rubbing my eyes

and stretching as Eloise bustled around my room, pulling drapes open and picking up stray articles of clothing. Eloise was the kind-but-strict, 50-something maid who was tasked with waking me, dressing me, fetching things for me, cleaning up after me- among other things around the castle.

Of course, I could dress and fetch things and clean for myself, so mid-yawn, I thanked and then guided Eloise from my room, gently reminding her I loved her, but she didn't need to help me dress, as I did every morning. She left with a sigh and a nod, frustrated that I kept her from doing her job.

I closed my door behind her and walked to my closet, yawning again.

I pulled jeans on, nearly falling sideways from being still half asleep. I changed my shirt, pulled my hair from the collar and tousled it lazily before leaving my closet. I walked back out into my room, which was, in my opinion, too big and over- done. But, I suppose, when you're living with royals, you realize everything's too big and over-done.

Me, I've lived at the castle all my life. Or at least, ever since I can remember.

I'm not the royalty, though, relax. I came from a tiny farm outside the city- or so I've been told. I just happen to be sort of close to the royal family- and always really close to one member in particular.

Kayleen is a sweet, trusting, golden-hearted, classic, funny little four-year-old princess. She's the only child of the Queen and the late King of Scarandia. She's my charge. I was assigned to protect her with my life. I'm sort of like a babysitter-bodyguard bound by a lifetime contract.

Let me explain before you get all appalled.

I am one of the **Protectors** that guard Kayleen. Every member of the royal family has four **Protectors**. Tayen and I were assigned to Kayleen when she was born, followed by Lanné and then Aaron when they turned eleven.

But we aren't just normal, stupid kids with a hand full of sword and a head full of pride. It's a bit more extraordinary than that.

A few months after children are born, there is a window in which there's an opportunity for their brain to realize its full potential. Every child is born with this suppressed spark- a specific gift- and when it wakes up, they either develop it or lose it. Few kids ever even notice it. And when they don't, life goes on- but if they do develop this spark, any dream or hope of being "normal, stupid kids" disappears in that instant.

When the power is first discovered, the child sometimes becomes a hush-hush deal. Not because the parents are ashamed- because they're afraid. Any child with a "gift" is taken away from the family and whisked off to the castle. Which isn't such a terrible life- except for the fact that the kid can never know anything of their past.

We don't know our parents, siblings. We don't even know our own last names. We lose our identity completely.

Well, I mean, theoretically, we're *supposed* to. We know some things we're not technically allowed to know, but then again, who doesn't.

It's a controversial and difficult job at times, but, hey, the benefits I get are the best in the country bar none.

Plus- I have a "superpower" or whatever, which is, apparently, pretty cool.

It's a bit complicated to explain, so pay close attention:

I can detach my mind and soul and spirit- whatever you want to call it- from my body, and go to another person's mind, see through their eyes. I see exactly what they see. I can also vaguely feel their emotions, too- it's like a tint, coloring their minds.

Talk about "putting yourself in someone else's shoes".

Everyone's minds are different- like their DNA. That's how I can track down the minds I want. The more I go to a person's mind, the more familiar their minds become- they're easier to find. It's like talking to someone, the more you talk to them, the more you know them, the easier it is to talk to them- I just take it a step further.

And another thing (and this is the really difficult part to explain) I can leave the person's head and walk around wherever they are- like a ghost. Or it's like my spirit travels, leaving my material body where it had been before.

It would compare to closing your eyes and vanishing out of your home and appearing in another person's house and then walking out their front door.

After I walk out the person's "front door" I become invisible to everyone and everything around me. No one can hear me or see me but I can hold and grasp real objects and people. People can feel my force, but if they tried to swipe at me, they would go right through me. I am exactly like a ghost in that state.

There is a dilemma: While I am walking around like a ghost-girl, my body is left empty- like a shell, a vacant house. All my body can do is breathe and blink and keep my heart beating. Someone could easily kill me by attacking my body while it's vacant. If someone threw my body off a cliff or stabbed it or- well, you can imagine your own examples- the effect would be the same for my "being"; my "ghost".

Long story short: if I want to, when I close my eyes, I can see- in *my* head what other people are seeing, or walk around with them like a ghost, but if anyone attacked my defenceless body I'd die.

Enough about me! As I said, there are four **Protectors** for every member. That leaves three more in my group.

Aaron, the youngest, is eleven- a funny kid but sometimes he's a bit immature. Scratch that- most of the time he's really immature. But I still love him.

Aaron can control matter. He can manipulate substances with his mind that otherwise would not be possible to control with human strength alone like fire, wind, copious amounts of water or extremely heavy things.

Well, he will be able to do all of that *sometime*. Sometime soon though- he's getting better!

Right now, he's basically telekinetic. Aaron can use his mind to lift everyday objects and unlock doors. His instructor says the brain is a muscle and Aaron's power acts the same way. Aaron has to work his way up to heavier, more complicated things from where he is. At the moment, water, air and fire give him trouble because the characteristics of the substance are relatively similar for his mind as they are for hands. Water is slippery, fire is hot and air is hard to control.

Aaron is a fast learner most of the time- the problem is that he's a bit impatient. Which is why his practices can go both ways: huge progress or absolutely squat. But that's just him- I'm sure it won't be a huge issue.

Lanné, the next oldest, is fourteen and she's... confident. Okay understatement of the year. She's cocky as all get out and grates on my nerves constantly. But the seldom seen soft side of her makes me melt. It reminds me that she does actually care. But that side of her makes an appearance once in a blue moon.

Anyway, she can **Scramble** minds. Her power is pretty self explanatory: she makes a person forget everything temporarily. Their name, who they are, where they are, their friends and family- everything. Absolutely, positively, one hundred per-cent everything.

It's really surprising to blink then

suddenly you don't know... anything... nothing at all. She's **Scrambled** my mind more than once, only for a little while but it's an experience that I do not highly recommend.

Tayen, the only other sixteen year old **Protector** I know, is quiet- he thinks a lot. He's rational, usually, and level-headed. Which is good, he balances me out well, I think it's why we're such good friends.

But basically, he can control bodies. The reason I say bodies and not minds is because the people can think for themselves and they know that they aren't controlling their movements anymore, they just can't say anything because Tayen has control of their jaws and keeps them shut. He can't control their vocal chords or tongue, so he can't make them speak what he wants, but I think he's working on that.

We aren't sure if he's limited to just humans, either, but we're still learning.

By *definition*, in *writing*, we are all

trained so that we learn how to *harness* and *suppress* our powers and *only* use them *limitedly* if ever a day came when we'd *need* them.

But in reality we're learning to fight because we're being trained to prepare for a war. No one says it out loud, but the whole castle is expecting an attack from Omen.

Omen is the Queen's younger brother, a traitor and a backstabber.

Omen believes that he should have the crown because he is the first son in the family. But it is stated that the eldest inherits the kingdom and only in the absence of the eldest can the next in line take over.

The Queen was the oldest of the two siblings, Omen followed after her and ever since he was able to comprehend the fact that she'd get the crown, he's been hell-bent on ruling the kingdom. When she actually became The Queen, he started trying to kill her. Then she married. Then she had Kayleen.

Which only made him more determined.

Just to clarify, it hasn't actually been proven that Omen was behind all the attempted murders, but all the facts point to him. It's just that no one would dare to accuse him of it.

Which makes me insane.

I would do it myself if anyone would listen to me. But what do sixteen-year-old kids know about conspiracy matters? What do sixteen-year-old kids know about anything?

Infuriating.

He murdered The King. I don't understand how anyone could ignore that. I mean, okay, he didn't literally stab The King with his own dagger or pull a trigger but I know he was behind the uprising- which was stopped before anyone could get to Kayleen or The Queen, thank the Lord.

Also, to make matters even better, The Queen is in denial. She won't accept the fact that Omen could have been behind it all. When her mother was dying, The Queen, still very young at the time, promised that she would keep Omen safe, too.

And since Kayleen is still alive, even if he managed to- God forbid- kill The Queen, Kayleen would still be in his way.

Now you understand why we **Protectors** exist: because of people like Omen.

Omen just returned to the castle a few weeks ago. No one knows what he had been doing when he left or where he went. But there's something different about him. I suspect he was gathering more followers and plotting another revolt. And I would even go so far as to consider that he'd **Created Spells** to tip the scales in his favour.

Only **Dark** people **Create Spells**. It's considered "cheating" sort of. But the **Spells** eat away at your soul. Every night, you are charged with the consequence of using the magic for evil. And eventually, the **Spells** will devour you from the inside out and you'll die.

I'm not sure what would happen to your soul if you used the magic for good, though- no one good has ever dreamed of trying because it has always just been considered witchcraft.

Besides, the materials are on a tiny, godforsaken island- not an interesting or popular destination for the people of Scarandia.

Scarandia is the island where the castle was built and was also where most societies today restarted from. Scarandia was the first island to be colonized since the Rebuilding of Time. The surrounding islands and communities for many miles around are all branches from Scarandia and are all ruled by The Queen. I'm just learning about all of this in my lessons- I guess this stuff did come in handy after all.

Scarandia is a huge island shaped like a crescent moon that is almost a complete circle. At the gates of the channel, the altitude is almost sea level but as you travel farther up towards the castle, plateaus and steppes lead to the peak, where the castle is set on top of the highest plain. The castle front looks out over Istallier Bay and behind the castle, beyond the grounds, is only cliff- a sheer drop-off. This cliff face actually curves inward- it's concave. So much so that if you were to look over the edge of the cliff, you would barely be able to see the thin sand strip below that surrounds the island.

I wondered if I jumped off the edge in my ghost-like state would it feel like flying?

Before I could consider giving it a try, Lanné met me in the hall.

# Chapter 2

"Kayleen's awake." She told me.

"Okay," I tilted my head to one side then the other, cracking my neck, making Lanné grimace.

I ignored her. "I was getting hungry anyway- you going for breakfast?"

"Yeah, but we're going to have to eat what's left over- Tayen and Aaron beat us there." She said. I rolled my eyes and sighed.

I followed her down the stairs that led from our wing on the second floor to the ground floor, paying no attention to the grand entrance as we passed it- which was a work of architecture that usually had people pausing to scoop their jaws off the marble floor.

The castle *was* beautiful, but I suppose after living in it for forever, I forget just how breathtaking the place is.

The ceiling of the foyer is around fifty feet above my head and the rows of tall, thin windows stretch some thirty feet up. Panes of stained glass at the top of each window bathe the sunlight in bright colors as it spills inside. A grand, split staircase leads to the second floor from where more stairs and corridors branch off to different wings and rooms and halls and towers.

We walked through the foyer between the split staircase and down the centre hall.

Rich, thick tapestries and huge, intricate paintings were hung wherever the wall was wide enough. Suits of armour from Kings past shine proudly against the sandy-grey stone walls. Red, velvet banners hang from the ceiling displayed the Royal Coat of Arms.

We made our way to the dining hall, and found Kayleen, Aaron and Tayen quickly, eating together near the head table.

"Morning," I said as I walked to the spot at the long table where we were sitting. Aaron and Kayleen were sitting on one side and Tayen was sitting across from them.

"Hi, Sirenna." Kayleen said, jelly smeared on her cheeks. She was swinging her short legs under the table and had her fist clenched around her fork, trying to stab a piece of ham.

Aaron grunted, his mouth full.

"Morning." Tayen nodded, not taking his eyes off his book.

At the head table, The Queen ate, politely engaging various lords between small bites of food. Her hands were light and fluttery and everything she touched it seemed, though it was heavy gold, became weightless as well.

Her body was angled away from a dark figure, shadowed beside his sister. Omen was staring blankly at his golden goblet, a tiny smile tugging at one corner of his mouth.

There definitely was something strange about him. He wasn't eating and if a person looked close enough there was a thin sheen of sweat crowning his forehead. His breathing was irregular.

As if he felt my gaze Omen lifted his eyes to me. His eyes were dark, set in a handsome angular face that gave me chills.

The bad kind. The kind that make a person wish they could puke in public places without creating a scene.

He put down his goblet without breaking eye contact and excused himself. Only when he stood to leave did I finally drop my eyes.

I nudged Tayen over so that I could sit down. He looked up at me and frowned slightly. I shook my head a minute degree then glanced up as Omen walked past on the other side of the table and nodded slowly at me, small smile still in place on his lips.

I shuddered as he left and then sat down by Tayen who slid a plate in front of me.

"Hungry?" He asked, his voice quiet, scarcely heard through all the chatter and clinking tableware.

"Not anymore." I grimaced.

Aaron hadn't stopped eating as he got shuffled over by Lanné to make room- I don't think he had even paused to breathe since he started. The kid was shovelling food into his mouth so fast it was like he'd never seen it before.

"Aaron- slow down or you'll hurt yourself." I said, picking up a fork.

"Yabuh I'mjisrullee hung gee." He replied, his mouth full of food.

"Swallow. Then talk." Lanné reminded him. He swallowed the eggs and toast with a very audible gulp, then reached for his glass of juice and chugged the rest- again very loudly.

He put the glass down, wiped his face along his arm and belched.

"Oh, God." Lanné mumbled.

I reached over the table and swatted Aaron. Kayleen giggled and Tayen just grinned and took another bite of toast.

"I said I was just really hungry!"
Aaron defended- a huge smirk on his face. I
rolled my eyes and began picking at my
breakfast.

# Chapter 3

"... when the first nuclear bomb ever made..." My history professor was going on and on. And on.

I was bored out of my mind. I was falling asleep and as my chin slipped out of my hand, Lanné reached her foot across and kicked me hard.

I glared at her angrily, then redirected my glare to the front of the room and tried to zone back in.

"...nuclear bombs were the starting point, the first step, if you will, that led scientists to the creation of the Disintegrade bombs. Disintegrade bombs were used during The Great Disaster. Now, the actual date of The Great Disaster, when the bombs were released was January the twent..."

My mind strayed from the lesson to the professor herself. She was short, squat, wearing a pink, tweed-ey skirt and jacket and shoes- all perfectly matched. She squeezed her eyes shut every time she blinked and, watching her blink-ey eyes, I noticed they were blue. Or green-

Green eyes... I glanced across the room at Tayen who was paying no attention to the professor either. His chin was rested on his crossed arms and he was staring at his desk. I smiled to myself.

"Sirenna!" The harsh voice of my

professor attacked my ears- which had automatically tuned her out, but her sudden, loud noise had broken the barrier.

"Yes?" I responded, caught off guard.

"Do you know the answer?"

I felt heat spread up my neck to my cheeks.

"I'm... I- no. I don't know." I sent daggers at the wall beside me through my eyes. The professor took another moment to give me a stern stare before picking someone else.

"Donnay?"

*Ugh, stupid Donnay. I hate him.* I growled in my head.

"The Disintegrade bombs were as powerful as *eighteen* nuclear bombs together." He said, his voice, clear and sharp, cut through the thick stifling air like nobody's business.

"Yes, Donnay, very good." The teacher praised. I could almost hear Donnay's smug grin directed at the back of my head.

"And it only took three or four of them to wipe out most of the world. The Great Disaster only lasted moments and everything was gone in an instant." She snapped her fingers, yanking my mind back to her lesson. "The impact of the bombs, as I'm sure you all know reshaped the landmasses and oceans drastically. You know what our map looks like today, well here is a diagram of what the map used to look like:" She unrolled a large map and held it up high.

I examined it and was hugely surprised at how big the land masses all used to be. I mean, the biggest continent we have is North Celendia. And that was even smaller than, like... North America? I squinted and leaned forward on my desk. North Celendia wouldn't even fill up...

Canada? Maybe it'd be the size of... Mexico...

The professor dropped her hands and began re-rolling the map, I sat back in my chair.

"Now," she sighed and kept on keepin' on. "The Dissintegrade bombs destroyed everything the people of the Information Age had accomplished." She set the map down but didn't stop talking. "Countless pieces of advanced technology were destroyed. Exploded to smithereens." Her arms extended in an imitation of an explosion.

I bet she practiced her lessons in the mirror...

"As well as thousands of years of knowledge, development and progress- all obliterated. Billions and billions of lives were lost but there were survivors." She paused to gesture around her. "Evidently- our ancestors. Now, we have restored some of the lost technology, but not all. Also, our societies didn't start completely from scratch- we have proper rights for minorities like women and different races, for two of many examples." She paused. "The survivors didn't get their minds wiped, everyone." She laughed. Nobody laughed with her.

"No," she cleared her throat, "civilization continued as best it could while the planet was in a dormant mode, repairing itself. That alone took hundreds of years before the Earth could properly sustain healthy life again. But once people began to rebuild communities, Scarandia was one of the first built. Which is why we have so much influence, internationally, today..."

I glanced errantly at Tayen again and my heart leaped when I saw him watching me. He grinned and hand-signed something to the effect of: "So freaking bored!" I smiled and just as I was about to respond, the professor wheeled to face me and she was mad.

"Sirenna! If I need to ask you one more time to pay attention-"

"I was! It's just- you just talk for so long it's hard to focus..." I trailed off, realizing what I'd said.

Her mouth gaped as she took in my words, turning bright red. "Leave my classroom, now." She commanded.

I ground my teeth and stood up from my desk and twirled out, grateful that my desk was the closest to the door in the class. I didn't bother staying to possibly get back in, there was minutes left in that class anyways.

I headed for the sports yard where I knew, a gruelling and elaborate obstacle course was set up and waiting for us.

*

\*                                        \*

The sun was beating down from right above me. Sweat was getting in my eyes and soaking my clothes.

I glanced across the hard-packed,

pebbly dirt to the green, green grass about twenty feet away. I moaned to myself at the thought of falling to my knees and then on my face on the soft, cool, green carpet.

But, regrettably, I was crouched in the ready position at the start line of yet another big, menacing monster of a course.

My muscles tightened and I focussed as the coach's assistant brought the whistle to his lips. I concentrated on my breathing, in, out, in... out... in.

My body sprang forward at the shrill noise of the whistle and I took off.

I hopped over the hurdles then dropped down onto my stomach and crawled under the hot, sharp, wire grid as quick as I could. When I was through I came to a long, wide, deep pit.

I knew what I was supposed to do. I **Sent** my sight into the nearest person's mind. Then I **Left** their head and I was free- I was bodiless. Like being a ghost. It was great. I glanced at my body, briefly. It was staring glossy-eyed, lifeless and still at the edge of the pit.

I ran as fast as I could and, without stopping, I jumped across.

In this state, when I jumped it was almost like flying- more like gliding. So I made it across the hole with room to spare.

I made my way to the big wheel. I turned the brass wheel until a tiny drawbridge lowered. When it was all the way down, I **Returned** to my body. I clamoured across the thin bridge. I dashed onto the long stretch of black rubber. A treadmill of sorts. Moving faster than I could run.

And when I say long, I mean looong. Not your basic one-hundred metre dash.

I stared longingly down the path. My throat burned and my mouth was dry, sweat was dripping down my face. If I could just catch my breath...

I remembered I was still being timed. I ran hard. As fast as I could on the counterproductive trail.

I finally came to the end and jumped onto stable ground, I sat crouched for a moment, one hand grazing the cool, gritty gravel, catching my breath. I sucked in the hot air, wishing in vain for a breeze.

Wait- *cool* gravel?

It took another moment before I realized I was standing in a big, blue shadow. I gathered my strength and pushed myself to stand and stare upward.

I had come to a tall wall. And they hadn't even been kind enough to provide me with handholds. I groaned. This course was way harder than the previous ones. My head hurt and I had a cramp from running so hard and I felt like my legs were going to give out on me at any moment. I was fed up.

I sighed and stumbled around the wall. I came to a stop in front of Bollen, my fat course coach.

"What's my time?" I asked, breathing heavily, wiping my forehead. He shook his ugly head.

"Don't count." He grunted.

"What!?"

"You didn't do the wall. Go back to the start."

This was not going to happen.

"Well, if I came across that wall in real life I *would* walk around it! I was just using my head! It's entirely valid!" I exploded angrily.

"No, go back." My coach pressed

I was prepared to throw myself into the pit until I remembered it still hurt a lot when you landed at the bottom, even though it was lined with a huge, squishy mat. Plus you had to climb all the way back out yourself, up a small ladder for about a hundred feet.

It was a tiring climb, I'd done it once before. They'd made me jump down into the pit the first time I used it so that I knew it was safe but draining and insanely maddening.

I stood there mouth agape, waiting for a brilliant, smart-alek response that never came from my exhausted mind. I was way too hot, sticky and sweaty, about to collapse- I was done.

But all I could do was turn around and go back to the start.

# Chapter 4

"I still think bedtimes are dumb."
Kayleen told me with a determined
frown...for the three thousandth time...

"I know, Kaylee, you told me last
time." My head and eyes drooped in
frustration. "But you have to go to sleep
now, you're growing and you need rest. And,

if you don't sleep you'll be an absolute monster and I'm not hanging out with you all day tomorrow if you're like that." I opened my eyes and she was yawning.

"See, you're falling asleep already, just lie down and close your eyes." I muttered, frowning

*Please, Kalyee, I'm tired, I'm achy and I just want to go to my bed and sleep right now!*

For the three thousandth time that night I had **Checked** on the princess, hoping to **See** her dreams, only to **See** her playing in her room. For the three thousandth time, I had trudged up the stairs to her room. For the three thousandth time, she had told me that she thought bedtime was unfair.

"I just think I don't need a bedtime! It's not fair."

Three thousand and one.

"Go to sleep or I'll get your mom." I

threatened. Her eyes widened.

"I thought you were on my team!" She cried, making me smile.

"No, I'm on my team and my team needs rest and I can't sleep 'till you're asleep so..."

"Okay." She nodded. "I'll go to sleep." She whispered.

"Good." I said, relieved.

"Can you tell me another story, though?"

"No."

"Okaaaaaaaay." She sighed and lay down on the bed and covered her head with the blanket. I kissed her head and stood up, my feet throbbing, knees weak.

"Sleep tight, kid." I said and I began to move for the door, when I felt eyes watching me. I spun silently, my heart racing-

But it was only Tayen, leaning against the doorframe with his arms crossed, grinning.

I let out my breath with a *whoosh*.

"Jeeze, why do you do that?" I whispered.

"Do what?" He frowned. "Goodnight Kaylee," He whisper-called.

"Night Tayen." She called back, sitting up again.

I glared at Tayen. He grinned at Kayleen and snapped. She giggled and put her head back onto her pillow. I stepped past him, slipping through the small gap between him and the doorframe, he closed Kayleen's door behind me and looked up but I was already halfway down the hall.

He caught up with me easily. I paused and looked up at him.

His wavy, blonde hair was just grazing his shining, green eyes. A flurry of butterflies flew around in my stomach. But I swallowed that feeling down and cleared my throat.

"So what do you want?" I stopped walking and crossed my arms.

"I just want to talk to you." He crossed his arms, too, but leaned close.

"People don't normally do that."

"Maybe they would if you would tuck away the sarcasm every now and then." He muttered, smiling, teasing. I wasn't amused.

"I had a bad day." I sighed, glaring at the wall.

"Clearly-" He raised his eyebrows and stepped back to walk away. Before I could stop myself I reached out and grabbed his hand, making him stop and he stepped close again, with another grin.

I looked down at my hand and yanked it back like it's been electrified.

"Well, it's partly your fault, getting me in trouble in history..." I muttered

"That wasn't all me." He said.

*Little does he know, it was him... distracting me- both times.* I thought. "Well, I'm easily distracted when she's lecturing like that." I muttered.

He laughed. "Don't blame you. Her class is-"

I frowned. "I'm sorry, for being... harsh-"

"*Harsh-*" He laughed, "wow, what an understatement-" he lifted his gaze up to the corridor wall, smiling, then back down at me.

"Okay, I'm mean, sorry. What do you want?"

He hesitated. "Yeah," Now he looked worried. "About that." I frowned. He started walking again and I hop-stepped to catch up.

"About..." I stared up at his face, trying to read his expression as we walked.

"I don't know exactly," he frowned deeply as he thought. His eyes flicked to me, "Don't laugh... at me... okay?" I nodded, and his eyes returned to concentrating on an image or thought in his head that I couldn't see.

"I feel like something's going to happen, a premonition, sort of."

I shook my head, ""Something's going to happen" wait- wha'd'you mean?"

"Have you caught anything... strange or different in anyone's mind lately."

He looked down at me and he was genuinely worried. I opened my mouth to say no but paused and searched my mind for anything odd, any red flag-

I shook my head. He sighed and we kept walking.

"I can't read minds, Tayen, but I'll **Watch** for weird things. Do the others feel premonition-ey, too?"

"I don't know, I don't... I haven't talked to either of them." He paused.

Lanné's... well, she might brush it off and we didn't want to offend Aaron, but, he was eleven, he's really young still. And to be honest, I felt responsible for him. We were all really close, us **Protectors** and Kayleen.

I saw us as a family; siblings. Kayleen would be the kid sister, Aaron would be the kid brother, Lanné would be the pain-in-the-butt teenage sister and Tayen... Well, actually, I don't know where Tayen fit anymore.

It was getting different, our relationship. We'd always been the closest.

He was my best friend- but now... More?

For example, when I grabbed his hand it was natural- normal- should've been no big deal. But now there was a different warmth where our skin touched. A different flash in his eyes. A different kind of race in my heartbeat.

There was something more.

But he couldn't be more- ever. I mean, I knew that, but at the same time...

I don't like thinking about it because makes me all confused and I hate it.

"It's late, we should both get some sleep." He said, interrupting my thoughts, and I realised we had stopped at my bedroom door. I nodded and sighed.

"Yeah, better be ready for another day, another class, another course. All the same... I wish something would change." I murmured.

I looked up at him and found that he was closer to me than I'd expected. I imagined electric sparkles flying across the short inch or two between us...

*Stupid, stupid- shut up! What are you thinking?* My inner-voice would've smacked me across the face if it could've.

He raised one eyebrow. "Careful what you wish for."

I'm sure he didn't mean to- but his extremely close proximity sent shivers down my spine.

See? Not normal.

"Yeah... Right." Was all I could get out.

I felt warm and jittery inside but at the same time I felt icy and empty.

But because I was falling for someone. Which is against the law for **Protectors**.

The penalty for breaking that law is death.

But a few short hours would quickly re-arrange my list of issues to tackle.

# Chapter 5

I was jarred awake by rough hands and a frantic whisper.

"Sirenna! Sirenna, wake up!"

"Wha-?" I blinked and peered out the window. Dawn was just barely leaking into the sky. I half opened my heavy eyes and felt around for a candle but before my fingers found anything, I was pulled up out of bed into the cold air. "'Kay just- calm down! Lemme get up an-" I started angrily.

"No, Sirenna. Move! Now!" I knew the voice- Tayen. His hands were too tight on my arms. I stared up at his dark figure in my room and finally clued in.

"Where's Kayleen?" I snapped, my mind kicking into hyper-drive.

"She's fine, for now. She's in the Council Room with Aaron and Lanné -" Tayen whispered hurriedly, chucking a pair of jeans at me. I booked it into the attached second room of mine where most of my clothes were thrown around.

"What's happening?" I asked, pulling on the jeans with one hand and yanking a bag stocked with food and other emergency stuff from a low shelf with the other. I swore, thinking about how I hadn't checked what was in there for a while.

"We don't have any time- we need to go. We got tipped off- someone spilled-" he continued as I pulled a thin, white, long-sleeved shirt over my head and grabbed my rust-red leather belt from a hook and fastened it around my waist. I pulled on one of my soft leather boots and then ran back into my room where Tayen was waiting, holding out a heavier, warmer, dark green tunic.

I snatched it and yanked it over my head. I grabbed my other boot from beside my bed and double checked that my knife was tucked inside its' hidden home- the secret sheath inside the leg of my boot. Then I pulled a box from under my bed, throwing the lid open and overturning it so that the contents spilled everywhere. I righted it, flipped up the false bottom and scooped out the shiny brass revolver and tossed it at Tayen. He caught it and chucked my cloak made of black weightless wool to me in return, and we ran out into the hall.

"*What* is going *on.*" I hissed as he fastened the revolver to his belt. He stared at me intensely, then- glancing around- he grabbed my wrist and dragged me down the hall.

*"Dammit,* Tayen, *what's going on*!?" I tried ripping my clenched fist from his vice-like grasp but he just yanked me back. He glared at me, hanging on to me tightly.

"Omen. And all his **Followers**." he murmured, loosening his hold on me, "that's what's happening." He slid his hand off my wrist to my hand and I clutched it as tight as I could, knuckles white.

# Chapter 6

We sprinted down the hall sliding around corners and practically flying down endless stairs. My surroundings were a blur of dark colours and streaks of light where the torches were lit. The only things solid in my world was the stone beneath my feet, the heavy strap of the emergency bag on my shoulder and Tayen's hand in mine.

All I could think about was Kayleen. The only thing going through my mind was "what if she got hurt...if she died", and I wasn't there to protect her because I was *sleeping*!? I didn't know what I would do...

This is what we've been waiting for, right? I thought I was prepared, but now it was coming all too soon.

I'd always assumed the worst when it came to Omen. So the icy fear grappling at my heart was as real and tight as my hold on Tayen's hand.

Omen was terrible, he wasn't afraid of anyone on this whole earth. He felt that he didn't answer to anyone, he was above everyone. He believed there would be no penalty for anything he did.

Soon, but not soon enough for my liking, we burst through the door of the Council Room and skid to a stop. All around me, people were piling in from the five doors that surrounded the room. Luckily, none of them were evil, just normal humans and The Queen's **Protectors**.

Some, I recognized but my eyes were for Kayleen and Aaron and Lanné only.

"Do you see Kayleen yet?" I gasped.

"No-" He pulled his eyes from scanning the crowd to scanning my face. "Sirenna, calm down, okay?" He caught my face in his hands. I was suddenly really annoyed with him- it felt like he was continually restraining me and I didn't like it, I started to pull my face away.

"Stop- touching me! Let me go-"

"Sirenna! Listen! Kayleen will freak out if she sees how you're acting right now." I froze, watching his face. He was right. "Jeeze, breathe. You're pupils are the size of marbles."

I obeyed and took a couple deep breaths and he lowered his hands and squeezed my shoulder before releasing me completely.

"Thank you." I allowed.

He looked away, scanning for Kayleen.

Lanné and Aaron appeared from the crowd and upon seeing us, came closer. Clutching tightly to Aaron's hand was Kayleen, who looked scared and sleepy. Both of them were carrying emergency bags of their own. I was so proud- all four of us had remembered, I realized.

A man began to speak loudly over the crowd, explaining the situation. I knew the voice, but under the current circumstances, I didn't care who it was, I just wanted Kayleen somewhere safe.

"The first order of business is your place, Queen." The man paused, waiting respectively for The Queen's answer.

"I am staying to fight, so are my **Protectors**." Her remaining two **Protectors** nodded.

The Queen had lost too many things in Omen's last revolt. Her husband, the King. Not to mention, six of the most awe-worthy **Protectors** I had ever seen. Two of The Queen's and all four of the King's before himself.

There was a tremendous crackling sound at the council room doors.

"They're here," I whispered to Tayen, my face draining of all the blood and my voice betraying how scared I was.

"It's alright, calm down. No one will do anything stupid, okay?" Tayen whispered back.

"We'll stay, too!" Called Aaron, to The Queen. Tayen froze.

I looked at Tayen with wide eyes, he murmured, "Of course, Aaron might-"

"No, you are taking Kayleen down into Brystone's Passage. Now." At The Queen's words, I glanced up at her. Another boom echoed through the air.

They say Brystone's Passage are a series of dark, stone tunnels and people have died in them because they could never find their way out again. These stories had been told to us as children but they were always told as folklore- old tales of mystery.

The Queen continued, "And you'll follow them as far as you are able, then you will climb out and run away from here until you collapse."

I saw The Queen's eyes fall on her daughter. I knew why we were running. As I said before, The Queen had lost too much in the last battle.

The hits were almost rhythmic now.

We were shoved from all sides, surging us forward out of the crowd, pushing us toward The Queen.

She pulled a tiny, rusty key and pressed it into a small keyhole in the ground. From the keyhole spread green cracks. No, a green light shone through spreading cracks in the ground. Whatever was happening- it looked as though we were all about to fall into some sort of blindingly, tech-neon-green cosmos.

I watched as the cracks spread then stopped and all connected to form a shining green square, carved deep into the previously seamless stone ground.

Suddenly the ground crumbled away leaving a perfect square hole. The rubble disappeared.

The council room doors began to splinter and the sounds of crazed men came louder now, through the breaking doors.

Tayen was the first to jump down, Lanné tossed him her bag then Aarons. People helped lower them both down into the tunnel.

The Queen bent down and kissed then hugged Kayleen quickly and I saw a tear slide down The Queen's nose. She wiped it away so subtly I almost didn't see her do it. She had to be strong for everyone else.

"Watch over her with your life, Sirenna." She said, the pain in her deep violet eyes was almost unbearable to see.

"Always do," I promised.

The Queen held Kayleen close again. "You do whatever Sirenna and the others tell you to."

"Mom-"

"And do not trouble over me, or anyone else. We will be fine." She smiled weakly, "we *will* be together again." She promised as arrows began to fly from the destroyed doors.

"But, mommy I-" The rest of her sentence was cut off when she was scooped up and lowered into Brystone's Passage. Then I felt hands, arms- rough, and solid. I was swept backward and pushed toward the entrance. I dropped down and stared back upward at the faces, the people.

The stone shone green again and began to reconstruct itself. As the last pieces assembled and the light dimmed, I saw a huge green-white flash and heard the hot *whoosh* of fire and splinters of the doors flew everywhere. The battle began as darkness closed in around us.

Screams, crashes, gunshots, dull thuds and the clatter of weaponry drifted to my ears through the solid, thick stone above us. They were all sounds that reminded me just vaguely of the clattering of silverware and countless voices chatting over breakfast this morning- our life so safe and stable.

And I had wished for change.

Footsteps. Scraping. Directly above us.

"Go! Go now!" I whispered and pushed Kayleen but she screamed and wouldn't move, she was crying. I swung her up into my arms and we all dashed down the black stone tunnel, Tayen grabbing my bag. Thank God the ground was level.

Above us, we could hear the sounds of a battle being raged, I only hoped we were the ones that were winning.

# Chapter 7

Brystone's Passage most likely wasn't named after its simplicity, though the name sounds simple enough.

After we had slowed our pace and stopped dashing through corridors mindlessly, we began to notice just how many splits in the path there were. Even if my life depended on it, I probably couldn't find my way back. That could work to our advantage, though, if anyone was following.

There was no hint of sunlight or anything from the above world at all anymore, now that the sounds had died away. Every ten feet or so there was a single candle mounted on the wall, a candle that burned blue. And we hadn't come across any candles that had burned out or even burned down, though there was no one to replace the candles or keep them lit. Which was eerie to say the least.

Every sound we made was magnified and echoed loudly down the dark, empty halls. Even when we didn't speak- every footstep, every rustle of fabric, every breath floated around us.

But that could also help us, too, we would be able to hear any pursuers- we'd be able to hear if we were being followed. The idea was haunting, to me- being slaughtered in Brystone's Passage. The chilling reality of this attack was just settling in, I guess.

"Sirenna, I'm hungry and cold, can we sit, please?" Kayleen's fingers were quite cold in my hand. I squeezed her hand.

"Sure, sweetie, that's a great idea. You guys?" I said in a hushed voice. The others agreed quietly.

At the darkest part of the tunnel- the farthest we could get from one light source while staying as far as we could from the other- we collapsed in a heap. Kayleen curled up by my knee while Lanné played with Kaylee's hair- Aaron against one shoulder, Tayen against the other. I sat against the stone wall staring at the blackness in front of me.

I tried again to **See** through The Queen's eyes, which normally is illegal, but since she was the only one that was really an important target, and in direct danger, I figured it was okay. I gritted my teeth and waited for the dark scene in front of me to turn into war, but it never did.

I had been doing this every few

moments for as long as we'd been wandering, always with the same results: nothing. It was like I forgot how to use my power. But that wasn't my biggest fear.

What I really feared was that The Queen was dead.

Well, I mean, really, I was most likely just tired. I usually jump to conclusions anyway. I would try again after I slept a bit.

Or I could try again now. Just in case.

I closed my eyes and willed myself to **See** The Queen. I was grinding me teeth so hard now, I was getting a headache.

Nope, nada.

I sighed in exasperation and listened to the annoying echo. I took another deep breath and let it out as silently as I could. I felt Tayen's hand close around mine again.

"How's everyone doing?" Tayen

asked. I opened my mouth, in the process of fabricating an ambiguous lie that would hide the fact that I couldn't **See** anything at all when Aaron sniffed and gurgled something quietly. I was caught off guard and realized he was trying to disguise the fact that he'd been crying.

I put my arm around him. "What?"

"Said I wanna go home." His voice was thick and quiet. After a pause, he whispered, "I wanna go back in time and kill Omen. Kill him-" Aaron's voice cracked and he sniffed again. "I want to rip his throat out. He deserves it."

Hearing this from an eleven-year-old, especially my eleven-year-old who has never had really violent tendencies- just mischievous ones that sometimes end violently- made my breath catch. It shouldn't be like this.

"Aaron we'll fix this, okay?" I squeezed his shoulders. "I promise."

# The Protectors: Once Upon a Catastrophe

# Chapter 8

We pulled the guts of our emergency bags out and arranged them on the ground. The contents inside my bag were different from those in Tayen's, Aaron's and Lanné's. I surveyed our equipment, to my extreme disappointment, we had enough food to last only about two days- *if* we rationed carefully.

Luckily, we had plenty of water for everyone, but it had been sitting in those canteens for who know how long. It tasted stale and smelled faintly of rotten eggs. But beggars can't be choosers, I suppose.

With the combined discovery of our lack of food and my personal distaste for the rank water, I made the executive decision that we would be surfacing as soon as possible.

That half comforted me and half scared me. I was happy that we'd be out of here soon, but afraid of being too close to Omen or his **Followers** when we emerged.

Other than food, we had four thin blankets, a poncho, some rope and a few more pocket knives, which we all armed ourselves with immediately. We also had two small bags of money, a pair of socks, two and a half pairs of mittens, a small, brass telescope, and a spider-spun gold chain with a tiny ruby pendant.

"Who's is this?" I picked up the

necklace, half expecting Lanné to claim it but she just sat there looking sad and more like a kid than I'd seen her in years. Actually we all looked that way. I tried not to look like that.

I was about to ask again when Kayleen spoke,

"That's mine, I figured if you were putting your things together, I should put something in, too, but that's all I had with me." Her voice dropped to nearly silent. "Mommy gave it to me. I usually never take it off but maybe it will help do something." She stared straight ahead and wrapped her arms around her knees.

"Kayleen- well- thanks, but, you don't have to hand over your possessions, sweetie, you keep it." I pushed the necklace back at her and she took it. Even though I knew she was trying her best to pretend it didn't matter to her, I saw the relief in her eyes when she clasped her hand around it.

Tayen sighed and spoke my words

before I had a chance, "Okay, well we've got enough food to last only a little longer, but if we're asleep we won't eat it, plus we need the rest. So, I'll take first watch."

I sent him a "you-bugger" look.

He peered at me in the faintest, flickering blue-ish light. "Go to sleep." He repeated.

I shook my head. Tayen let out an exasperated sigh and mumbled. "Stubborn".

*Well, he can think what he wants,* I thought, *but I need to talk to him.*

I figured I'd wait 'till the others were asleep, then we'd talk.

I glanced around, Kayleen was snuggling up to Lanné who was trying to comb the knots out of Kayleen's hair with her fingers. Lanné always played with hair when she was stressed out. Kayleen just looked tired. Aaron was curled up in a ball, swathed in a blanket cocoon, but his eyes were open and wide.

Everyone was tense. It'd be a long wait before they fell asleep, but I needed to talk to Tayen.

# Chapter 9

Another man rushed at Omen from the crowd. Omen raised his hand and from it, a fireball erupted and sent the man flying. He slammed against the wall and then slid to the ground, leaving a trail of blood painted fifteen feet high.

Omen stalked through the fighting

to the next attacker. He pulled the man's sword out of his hands by the blade ignoring the sharp slicing sting.

He clubbed the hilt against the man's head. His head began to bleed and he stepped backward away from him. Omen's eyes were fixed on the man's- burning the guard's mind.

He shrieked as his mind seared inside his skull. He raked his fingernails down his face trying to claw out the fire. Omen ceased the burning in the man's mind and kicked him on his back and ground the hilt of his sword into the man's eye socket.

He was thrashing wildly now, shredding his hands on the blade as he tried to fight Omen.

Omen cocked his head and jerked the sword sharply out of the gaping, bleeding hole. He twirled the sword, caught it and stabbed the man's stomach, cutting it open. Omen dropped the blade with a clatter and left the man to collect his intestines in time to be kicked and trampled to death by other fighters.

Omen smiled, surprised as a young boy- perhaps in his twenties, with long dark hair and a softly featured pale, white face- confronted Omen. He was quivering slightly, but he had a determined look on his face.

He took a deep breath, raised his arm and held his revolver tightly. His hand was shaking violently.

Heart racing, he pulled the trigger and the device made the worst sound a gunman could possibly imagine hearing; a quiet mechanical click and then nothing.

The boy's face drained of blood and he stared open-mouthed at the gun in his hand, the one he'd forgotten to reload before facing the most dangerous enemy he'd ever encounter.

He looked up at Omen's smile, a deceivingly kind grin that sent ice-cold liquid fear running down the boy's spine.

He glanced back at the revolver and watched it fall to the ground, the small gears and screws jamming as it hit the stone floor. Omen caught the boy by the throat before he could run away and pulled him close.

The boy's eyes started to tear. He tried to look away, close his eyes, anything- but he couldn't break Omen's gaze.

Omen smiled. He forced his fingers in the boy's mouth, ignoring the quiet pleas for mercy. This was mercy.

With a loud crack, Omen ripped off the boy's jaw, sending him spinning to the ground and screaming. Omen knelt down in front of him, his violent sobs shaking his whole frame, blood pooling on the ground.

"Here," Omen said softly, soothingly. "You dropped this."

He threw the boy's jaw on the ground in the pool of blood before him and then heaved him off the ground, pulling him up by his slick, bloody neck.

The boy held himself standing long enough for Omen to, in one swift motion, snap his neck and let him die.

The body fell with a thud and Omen turned, his expression indifferent.

No more men attempted to stop him.

Men were cowards.

But men were not his target at the moment.

He wanted to find his big sister.

*

*                                    *

Finally everyone was asleep, except Tayen and me.

I slid over to where he sat motionless, alert, listening for footsteps.

"Sirenna, I can handle watch alone

for a few hours." He whispered, frowning.

"I know, I know you can," I whispered back, putting my hand on his arm. "But I need to talk to you-"

"No, you need sleep," He stared at me intensely for a moment, then the intensity faded to confusion.

"What are you doing!?" He muttered, alarmed.

I frowned, "I'm not doing anyth-"

"I know- that's my point- Right now, you should be stuck on the floor with your mouth shut and your eyes closed... I don't understand what-"

"I know, that's what I wanted to talk to you about." I whispered, "I was going to say that I couldn't **See** anything- my power isn't working either."

Tayen frowned, "Why didn't you tell me this earlier?"

"I didn't want Kayleen to be scared." I explained, my voice a near inaudible.

We both glanced at her, breathing quietly, eyes closed, mouth open a little.

"What do you think it is?" He asked.

"Well, I tried to **See** and I couldn't. I considered maybe I was shaken up and needed to calm down. But I've been trying all night and still, nothing. So when I still couldn't **See** The Queen... I assumed she was-"

"Dead." He whispered brokenly.

I looked up at him and after a moment, shook my head.

"No. It doesn't make sense. She had **Protectors**- and the rest of the castle watching out for her. She can't be gone."

"So did the King..." He reminded me.

"Tayen. She isn't gone, I know it, I

just don't know why I can't-"

"Sirenna, maybe your first theory was right. Maybe you're just spent. You *need* to sleep. Get some rest while you can."

"But I-"

"Shh."

I frowned.

"Fine."

I leaned my head against the cold wall of the Passage and curled up under a cloak. For the first time that night, or morning- I didn't know what time it was- I felt how heavy my limbs and eyelids were. I gave in and tried, unsuccessfully, to let my muscles relax.

*He is right, I suppose,* I thought, *I mean, who's to say this isn't one of Omen's tricks. Once I get some rest, and I can think clearly- once we get far enough away from Omen we'll be alright...*

*But how could this be Omen's fault? And if it affected us all then... it would affect the other **Protectors**... wouldn't it?*

I opened my eyes, my breath catching in my throat at the realization. Tayen heard my breathing falter and shifted his gaze to me again.

"What's wrong?"

"I think I know..." I whispered, looking up at him.

"Yeah..." He urged.

"I bet it's Omen. I bet he made a **Spell** that throws off our powers. Tayen," I looked up at him, "don't you remember? It was The Queen's **Protectors** that stopped him last time, right? And they stopped him with their *powers*. Omen would be sure that that couldn't happen again..." My voice trailed off and I looked at Kayleen. "But then... They don't stand a chance..."

Realization dawned on Tayen's face.

He stared at me silently.

I bit down on my lip and tasted blood as tears started prickling at my eyes. Tayen pulled me close and hugged me. He stroked my hair and I let a few tears fall for everyone who would die tonight.

# Chapter 10

Omen's desire to destroy his sister and take her kingdom grew with every empty room he discovered. He was getting tired of searching for her, wandering through everything that should have been his for years.

He turned his head when he heard

the dull thud of a body falling. He stepped around the corner into a lavishly furnished room and smiled.

She stood proud and undaunted by his presence.

"Omen," The Queen murmured quietly, as she wiped her sword on a plush chaise.

He raised his eyebrows, no one had dared call him by his name for a while now. It was refreshing.

The Queen continued. "What are you doing-?"

"Taking what was rightfully mine." He saw her flinch an infinitesimal bit.

"You would do all of this for the crown?"

"I know what I'm doing. Now it is time for you to choose." Omen muttered. "I am prepared to fight until every last one of my men are dead. How about you?"

"But, what about the families you are destroying?"

"Family is useless. A pointless excuse to make life painful and excruciatingly grating. They are better rid of it."

The Queen glared at him with dark, wary eyes. Omen continued.

"Listen carefully- I will not repeat this: give me the crown or I will remove it from your severed head." Omen pronounced every word slowly and carefully.

"You wouldn't kill your sister-"

"Sister? What does that matter? For all I care, I have no sister. All you did was ignore me, push past me, you think you're better than me still. You look down on me. How does that exempt you from this?" Omen growled, "I will kill anyone in my path, anyone who will get in my way. You are no exception."

"Omen, you can't be so cruel, that's-that's evil."

"I know." He smiled.

The Queen took a deep breath and set her jaw.

"This is not a game and I've grown tired of playing along. Omen, you will *not* have my throne. I will *not* give in."

Omen flicked a long sword of green fire into his hand. He attacked and she blocked, his sword met hers and sparks flew on contact. The Queen's eyes grew wide as she saw him holding the flame.

"Impossible!" She whispered.

"Are you afraid?" Omen asked. The Queen didn't speak.

"Fear makes you weak." He spun out and swung his sword at her waist but she blocked it. He spun around the other way and tried to hit her head but she blocked that, too.

He lunged and swiped around her everywhere. But at every blow, his sword met steel.

Finally, he got impatient, again. He made easy and predictable moves. He went faster and faster, stepping closer each time. The Queen's eyes showed panic and fear as she blocked every hit and sparks were everywhere, a spark caught on an old tapestry and the flame spread like a grassfire.

Then, he aimed at the hilt of her sword and it flew out of her hand. His sword vanished. He punched her in the mouth, and the surprise that registered on her face was pure and unmasked. Her lip was bleeding and she was shaking.

He pulled her off the ground and wrapped his long fingers around her neck.

"This is your *last* chance, Anastasia, give me your crown and you've live." He looked into her eyes as she gasped for air. "Whether living is a good thing, I'll let you decide-"

"Omen, let go of me! I can't breathe!" She scrabbled at his hand, leaving deep gouges in his skin as she struggled for air.

He squeezed his hand and lifted her off the ground, shoving her against the wall, flames from the burning tapestry licked the side of her face and singed her hair.

She choked and gasped and Omen watched silently until the light in her eyes began to dim. He pulled his lips back in a snarl.

"Give up Anastasia. You've lost, don't drag this out." He muttered.

Omen let her go and she fell to the ground, lying still where she landed.

Black smoke began to curl around the room as the fire spread from one piece of furniture to the next.

He bent down and pulled the spindly crown from her hair and stared at the thin, golden web that was created by the intertwining metal. His fingers tingled and he grinned.

He was The King.

# Chapter 11

The fire raged and spread around her, but The Queen waited until Omen had left, and as long as she dared after he had disappeared before she lifted her head.

She winced at the movement, rubbing her throat. She knew she needed to disappear, and fast.

The heat had begun to stifle her and the smoke billowed out of the room thick and black.

The Queen crawled behind a long, blue couch and pressed against the back of the piece. She was choking and her eyes were watering.

How was she going to get out unnoticed?

The rooms surrounding her were unoccupied, as far as she knew, as were the surrounding halls.

The castle was deserted. If she could get the council room without being found, she could get into Brystone's Passage and get out.

She hated herself for leaving her castle and people, but she'd be back. If she told anyone that she was still alive, the news would get out and Omen would be after her again.

Best to leave without anyone knowing, she'd explain to her people after Omen was dead.

She winced, again, at the thought of having to kill her brother. Maybe she didn't have to, maybe she could put him in the blank room. This room had no windows, only one door with no handle on the inside and nothing he could use to break out.

Except his magic. He could probably blast out in no time and go on another rampage.

No, he'd have to die. Besides she had already bent the rules for him once. She couldn't do it again.

She crept out from behind the furniture, scooping up her sword along the way. She peered at the blade. It was all chipped and notched.

She slipped out of the room and covered her mouth with her hand. Tears welled up in her eyes. *What's he done to my home!?*

The walls were all broken and there were people lying everywhere. She didn't look at the faces, since most of the bodies were her guards. The beautiful paintings and tapestries that used to hang on the walls were ripped and ruined, lying on the ground. What was left of the gorgeous red, velvet banners were smouldering or still aflame in a heap on the floor. There were no living people around.

It was a deserted war zone.

Suddenly, she couldn't take the terrible sights any longer. She dashed to the staircase and ran down the endless stairs to her room. Which, of course, seemed to take longer than usual.

She finally arrived at the grand foyer. She poked her head out and scanned the whole area for anyone living. There was no one. She stepped out and, running silently, made her way through the blood and bodies and fire to the council room.

At one of the corners she rounded, she felt icy nausea take hold of her at the sight of two figures at the end of the hallway. She pulled back and flattened herself against the wall. Suddenly she heard the voices rise. More voices shouted.

*They saw me- they saw me, they'll take me to Omen-* She thought, slipping away from the corner.

"You two!" She heard a distinct voice call angrily. "state your loyalties to th..."

*No,* she paused and listened.

She caught bits of words that the voices were saying:

"...attendance..."

"...decree of The King-"

"My King is dead..." The man said, voice growing louder. "He has been dead for a long time... killed by that traitor you worship-" The Queen squeezed her eyes shut. The people were her followers.

"Omen is the King." The angry voice got louder.

"I'll attend your king's ceremony... If only to *kill* him *myself*." The other voice countered, spitting the word "king".

Swords clashing. The Queen's heart beat faster- risk being seen, being caught? Help her people?

A man cried out. The explosive *crack* of a revolver shot shattered the sounds of the fight.

The Queen rushed around the corner to watch a man clad in black slip down a hallway, three dead bodies on the ground.

The one who was stabbed was another dressed in slithery black- Omen's man. The Queen paid no attention to him, she fell in front of the other two forms on the ground.

One was still breathing shakily, face ashen and pained.

"Soldier. My brave soldier, what is your name? Can you tell me your name?" The Queen coaxed the dying man, clasping his hand.

"My- Q- Queen? Is- is-? *Ahh-*" He squeezed his eyes shut tight and then opened then wide, gasping.

The Queen smiled through tears. "I'm here." The man tried a shaky smile. Genuinely happy to have her near.

"J- J- Jeromiah. My- my name."

"Jeromiah. Let's see what we have-" The Queen moved to examine the man's bullet wound, a gaping, burning hole in his chest. The coward had shot him point blank.

"No- no!" The man protested The Queen's hands "It's- it's my time- I can feel- feel it-"

The Queen choked as she tried to console him. "You've fought so valiantly -"

"F- for- you. My- my Queen-" He smiled and then winced, cringing at the pain.

"Shh- shh- be at peace. May God rest your soul and watch over you, my Jeromiah." The Queen held his hand tightly as the man succumbed and fell still, his shallow, laboured breaths dying away.

The Queen squeezed his hand and touched it to her forehead. In a way, mourning for all her lost people. Fighting for her. Fighting for freedom.

At the sound of approaching voices and footfalls, The Queen lurched to her feet and looked around. She gave a last parting look to Jeromiah, so quiet, as if he were sleeping, and then disappeared around the corner into the council room.

Digging in her pocket, she pulled the small key once again and pressed it into the hidden lock in the ground. She glanced nervously around as the passageway opened up.

She grabbed a burning torch from the wall and lowered herself into the tunnel. The stone sealed itself with the same green glow, swallowing her up, trapping her beneath her home. So close yet so far away.

So far away. With Omen as King and her baby missing and all her people dead above her. It was so far from being her home.

She prayed her people would take her back. If she was ever able to come back. But first, she'd find her little girl, then deal with Omen.

# Chapter 12

"Sirenna, Lanné's right- we gotta leave this place, I don't like it here." Kayleen said quietly, listening to her scared, tiny echo. Lanné nodded.

Lanné and I were arguing about whether or not we should try and find our way out of Brystone's Passage. Yeah, we would run out of food soon and yeah, we all wanted to get out of here but, I thought rest was a better idea first.

Plus, my point of being a leader didn't hold much water since I wasn't really, officially the leader, just the oldest.

"I wanna see the sun and the sky and stuff, too." Aaron added, yawning.

We had slept for what felt like a few minutes before Lanné woke us all up, wanting to leave.

"Wait, look. That's my point." I said, pointing at Kayleen's hunched posture and Aaron's droopy eyes "I think we need more rest and food-"

"No, Sirenna! We have to *leave* to get food and a good place to hide so that we can be safe from Omen!" Lanné was quiet, pausing for effect and I waited patiently. "I mean, if they find a door... This is a direct connection to the castle-"

Kayleen whipped her head around to stare at Lanné, "They could find us!?" she breathed, glancing back at me, worry in her big, violet eyes.

"No, Kayleen, they won't find us." I turned and glared at Lanné. "and it's not a direct connection, it's a confusing labyrinth of underground tunnels. There's no way they could-"

"What about tracking devices?" Lanné interjected.

"Lane- cut it out, we don't need you upsetting everyone even more than we already are." Tayen said from behind me.

"Thank you." I sighed and walked toward him.

"But, Sirenna, we *should* leave..." He added in a low voice.

"Oh, you've *got* to be kidding!" I snapped and spun on my heel, walking back to the centre of the circle. I crossed my arms and thought, everyone watching me.

What's the worst outcome? What would be the best for Kayleen? What are the pros and cons of both situations?

These were the questions they taught us to ask ourselves... none of them were easing the decision-making process right now.

"Fine, you all win." I muttered, lowering my arms. Aaron punched the air with his fist and Lanné smiled widely. I was extremely frustrated.

Not only had I just been proven wrong- which I hate- I had no clue where to start looking for a way out. And to add to the problem, I couldn't measure how far from the castle we were. But no matter where we were or what was happening, we had to get above ground eventually.

I focussed and concentrated on the current task at hand. Finding a way out would no doubt be complicated, these trails were spider webs. If I wasn't paying attention, we could spend the rest of our lives walking in circles.

We started off again, despite my hesitation, nausea and bad feeling-ness.

As we left the light of the strange candle behind us, I felt like running back- even though the glow was anything but comforting.

But at least it was brighter than the overwhelming shadow that was lying ahead.

# Chapter 13

Something touched my arm. It was Tayen.

"Do you have any idea how we're going to get out of here?" He whispered in my ear.

"Not the slightest. You got one,

Brilliant? It'd be more helpful if you shared it."

"Well, we dropped down into these tunnels, and we haven't gathered any sense of an incline, so I'm assuming the exit would obviously have to be above us."

"Obviously." I agreed.

"And if it's just like the entrance back in the castle, it'll be locked." He pointed out, presenting our next obstacle.

"Great. And that requires a key, which we're lacking." I sighed.

"I noticed." He said dryly.

"Solution?"

"Niente."

"Very helpful." I muttered sarcastically.

"Maybe they're not all the same,"

suggested Aaron, "the entrances."

"Thanks for inserting yourself into the conversation, there, Aaron." I frowned.

"I was eavesdropping." He said, his tone was layered with surprise at the fact that we hadn't already assumed that. In all honesty, it wasn't exactly surprising.

"At least he's honest." I mumbled under my breath before I turned to Lanné, knowing she was in on this conversation too, by now. "Lane, any ideas?" I asked.

"Uh, well, what if it's like a lock on one side- only the above-ground side-"

"We're locked in here?" Kayleen asked.

"No," she thought for a moment. "But, maybe it would open from this side without a key or anything-"

"And how exactly would that work, Lanné?" Aaron retorted, cutting her off.

"Guy! Don't start with the bickering-" Tayen began.

One minute I was thinking intently about the possibility of Lanné's theory and the next thing I knew, something was grabbing on my leg and I crashed to the floor.

You can believe me now, I honestly don't fall on purpose. Though recently, my track record might suggest otherwise.

I turned and scrabbled up the stairs to get away from the thing that grabbed me. I stood up and prepared to tackle the creature and when I realized, nothing was grabbing at me, I had tripped over the stair that I landed on.

*Oh! Stairs!* I thought, excitedly.

"Are you alright?" Tayen asked.

"I'm fine, but look- I found stairs!" I grinned, back at them in the flickering light of the candles.

# The Protectors: Once Upon a Catastrophe

# Chapter 14

The stairs lasted all of six steps.

When we reached the end of our stair-journey, we knew it. What tipped us off? First clue: A solid wall.

Guess how we found it- no I'll just tell you: we ran into it. Well, Tayen did.

"Ow! Mother-"

"Hey! *Blah! Blahblahlalalaaaaaa!*" I yelled as Tayen started swearing. I let go of Kayleen's hand as I passed Lanné and Aaron, reaching around in the dark trying to find him.

"I didn't expect that... Jeeze-*uh!* That *hurt!*" He hissed.

"What's wrong? Why're you-"

Tayen grabbed my outstretched hand and pulled me toward him, his hand holding my wrist. He guided me in front of him.

I swayed, nearly losing my balance in the dark and he lightly held my waist to steady me. I got chills, but strictly shook the sensation off.

"What? What's the matter?" I asked, focussing my mind again.

"Well- look." Tayen's hands had

dropped from my waist and his voice came from beside me. I reached out in front of me, expecting cold, empty air again but instead, my fingers rammed up into a stone roof.

"What!?" I breathed, in disbelief, "Why is this here!? No one puts stairs that lead to nothing." My hands whipped around the roof, feeling for a handle to pull, but only found more stone.

"Apparently whoever built this tunnel did." Tayen mumbled, still miffed about the new goose-egg that'd probably appear soon, doled out by the *solid wall.*

"That doesn't help, Tayen." I growled.

I put my hands down slowly, feeling empty, I stopped and was about to turn when the stone above me began to crack. I backed up, two quick steps that almost sent me falling backward down the stone stairs. A silver light was streaming in through the cracks. *What? What'd I do?* I thought, looking up.

The stone roof was now hovering, a few feet in the air. I narrowed my eyes in confusion then slowly faced Aaron, who's grin was so big I wondered how he fit it on his face.

"Are you doing that?"

"Yup!" He smiled wider.

I grinned back and mussed up his hair. "What would we do without you, kiddo?"

We all pulled ourselves out into the cool, fresh air, the moonlight beaming down on us. I took a deep breath, chasing all the old musty air from the tunnels out of my lungs.

"Could you have done that the whole time we were down in Brystone-?" Lanné asked.

"I was trying to, but my powers wouldn't work, so I gave up. Just now, though, I tried again, and it worked!" His face shone and I half expected him to throw his hands up and shout, "Ta-daa!".

"Tayen!" I snapped my eyes onto his, mine wide and excited, his were surprised and defensive.

"What!?" He countered, half mocking my excitement and half caught off-guard.

"That means our powers are back!" I said, excitedly.

"Oh, thank God!" Lanné muttered with a sigh. We turned to stare at her, "I thought I was going crazy." She sighed, relieved.

"You were trying to scramble our brains!?" Tayen growled at her, his face slowly turning to glare at her, "as if it wasn't hard enough down there?" He gestured back toward the opening to the tunnel, which Aaron was sealing again. "Who's brain were you trying to mess with, anyway?"

Aaron looked frustrated at the lack of attention we were expending on his amazing feat.

Yeah, it would be amazing for any normal person, but for a kid that used his power to dress himself in the morning, lifting dirt wasn't that astounding.

I suppose, he did get us out of Brystone's Passage...

*Memo to self: give Aaron a little more credit for saving our hides*, I noted. The escalating conversation yanked me out of my thoughts:

"I was bored! There was nothing else to do down there!" Lanné was defending herself loudly. Tayen looked ready to strangle her.

"Guys, stop! It doesn't really matter what she was going to do, 'cause she didn't do it!" I directed that comment at Tayen, "Besides, we're out of there anyways! We're here!" I smiled at Aaron and Kayleen and looked around.

"But where's "here", though?"
Kayleen asked me. *Uh, yeah,* I thought,
glancing around, myself, *now where are we?*

# Chapter 15

I turned a full circle, trying to get my bearings. Obviously, we were in a forest, but it was the strangest forest I'd ever been in.

The trees were thin and spaced far apart and there were no branches until high up, way past our heads. The ground was flat, no roots poking up, and no little trees or shrubs. It was like the giant, skinny, tall trees had sprung up from a carpet of moss. It was so odd.

Also, there was no sound- none. Until now, I hadn't noticed how quiet it was, there was no wind rustling leaves, no animal sounds, no birds calling. It was an eerie effect. There was even a light dusting of fog- how cliché.

I was tempted to turn our troop around and march our sorry, scared butts right back into Brystone's Passage.

Well, maybe not, but almost.

*Alright, I'm getting nowhere,* I thought to myself.

I sighed, in defeat, and rubbed my eyes. "Does anyone have any ideas concerning *where* on this entire island we might be?" I asked, opening my eyes again to see everyone shake their heads, no.

"We should just start walking, at

least," Aaron suggested, "Right? I mean, does it matter where we are? We still need food and a place to stay." I nodded.

"Yeah, let's walk, we'll come across something eventually that'll give us an idea." I started walking. No one followed me, I paused and turned to face them again. "C'mon, guys- Aaron, it was your idea-"

"Shh!" Tayen put a finger to his lips.

"Don't "shh" me!" I hissed, narrowing my eyes.

"Shut up!" Lanné hissed right back at me. My mouth fell open, I closed it, locking my jaw and I waited.

"Good job, Sirenna, now we don't know what it is!" Lanné shot at me.

"What *what* is!?" I asked, exasperated. Tayen motioned for me to zip it again. I sighed, watching Tayen survey the area.

"Something made a noise, Sirenna," Kayleen whispered and grabbed my hand, "I'm scared." Her worried face stared up at me.

"Hey, it's okay, it was probably just the wind, 'kay?" I squeezed her hand. Tayen was still scanning the woods, slowly.

"No, it growled, Sirenna, I heard it!" She whimpered.

"We'll keep you safe, Kaylee, I promise." I promised and rubbed her arm.

"Sirenna I heard-" Aaron started but paused. This time, I heard it too. It was a low, throaty growl, almost a purr, that lasted only a second, then the woods were quiet again.

"It came from over there," Tayen whispered pointing past me, I turned around and scanned the ground as well. Nothing.

"Let's walk," I gently nudged Kayleen. She shuffled ahead a few steps and stopped again. I sighed and walked out in front of her, dragging her just slightly. I wanted to get away from whatever was growling.

Lanné and Aaron grabbed the two bags we had left and we started walking. As we drifted through the trees, I glanced at Tayen.

His bright green eyes shifting all around us, watching for danger. His hair looked pale and silvery in the moonlight and his skin looked like white marble. His muscles were tense, his fists clenched. A tiny smile tugged at the corner of my mouth.

I got a sudden urge to shout "BOO!" at him, and watch him jump five feet in the air, but then I remembered we weren't just playing around in the castle anymore. Y heart sunk again.

As I watched him, I saw the tree beside him quiver. I jolted my sight up to the top of the tree. There was nothing.

Aaron's keen brown eyes caught my

movement, "What's wrong, Sirenna?" He asked. I looked down at him and let the muscles in my face relax.

"Nothing, Aaron," I messed up his dark brown hair and smiled, "Just watching stuff." Aaron gave me a grimace and put his hair back the way he liked and glanced away.

Tayen could tell I was lying- he stared at me, concern and question on his face.

"The trees." I signed to him.

He shook his head, and mouthed: "What?"

Then the tree beside me quivered, too and everyone's eyes shot to the top of that tree.

*What is going on?* I screamed in my head, angry. There was nothing in the tree again.

A branch fell from the trees and landed in front of Tayen, making him pause. He only had time to look down at it, with a frown before a big, black mass of snarling fur and claws jumped out from the top of a tree landed on Tayen's back, pushing him to the ground.

It leaped off him and skid to a stop some feet away, leaving deep gouge marks in the moss and turned to face us, snarling. Tayen looked up as the creature jumped at him again.

Lanné grabbed Kayleen and dashed away with her as Aaron and I flew into action, attacking the monster.

I was already in motion before I had even thought of moving. I dashed at the black beast, but it had its sights on Tayen. It collided with me as it blew past, running at Tayen. The force sent my spinning, falling, about six feet from where I'd been standing.

Tayen jumped to his feet and braced himself as the animal leaped at him, teeth bared. The huge, heavy creature was part dog part monkey part fricken' bull, I don't know how else to describe it.

It knocked Tayen backward again, with a strong flick of its head. Then it was on top of him, jaws snapping.

Aaron was trying to get a safe, clear shot at the monster so he could hurl any stray heavy objects that were lying around, but there were none and at this point if he sent anything in the creature's direction, he'd hit Tayen.

Tayen, who was straining to hold the creature's neck while it tried to bite his face off, took the chance of reaching for his gun but quickly thought better of it when he almost lost the wrestling match with the snarling, drooling mass of sharp teeth and claws.

# Chapter 16

"I know it was you, Caytos." The young boy quivered before Omen, blood running down his face. "You were supposed to bring the Queenling to me and you let them go."

Omen stood and circled the man, moving silently, a shadow. His cloak billowing behind him like the black wings of death.

"There is no escaping me. I know lies when I see them. I *am* lies. I am the living example of betrayal. The Queen is the symbol of the betrayed. I will not be like my her. I will not be blind, Caytos." Omen said, quietly, the velvet of his voice soft and deadly.

"It wasn't me, Highness, I swear, Highness-"

"*Liar.* How *dare* you taint words to my ears with your *filthy lies*!"

"No, Sir!" The man shook violently, his voice cracking.

"*No*? Insolent cyst-"

With a flash Caytos' body collapsed, convulsing. His screams pierced the air, a million daggers to the ears of anyone nearby. Another flash and the shrill screaming stopped.

His body lay still on the ground in a pool of blood. His head twenty feet away, features still twitching in a mask of blinding pain.

"How did you know it was him, Sire?" Ventured Zerago.

"I didn't." Omen muttered. "That is not why he is dead." Omen turned his cold eyes to his sideman. "He told me *no*."

# Chapter 17

I pulled out my revolver and took my aim, but the thing was just too damn close to Tayen- if I hurt him, I couldn't live with myself. I didn't like guns.

With a loud, angry, frustrated *gahhh!* I chucked the gun aside and sprinted towards the monster and slammed into it, hard, pushing it off Tayen. It was heavy but really skinny, I could tell it hadn't eaten in a while.

Oh, *that's* why it was attacking us- it figured we looked like tasty, delivery dinner packs. All the nutrients and vitamins it needed, rolled into five neat, compact, convenient snack bites.

Well, I had never really shown a keen interest in being involved in the foods industry... let alone being the *food* part.

It fell sideways, off Tayen, and crashed hard on the ground. I landed on top of it.

It jerked and I felt a scorching hot slice across my back as it snagged me with its long, ragged claws. I cried out and smashed my fist into its neck. It twisted and kicked me off.

I was catapulted off the animal with unnatural force. I slammed into a tree sideways, my head smashed against it. My back seared and I couldn't breathe and my head pounded. The world spun and I had double vision.

The animal loomed closer. I swiped at the canine-like snout but missed. The creature's muscles coiled as I tried to clear my head.

Suddenly, the animal squealed and jumped back, Tayen had kicked the side of its head. He had the branch that had fallen from the treetop and started clubbing the animal's face with the heavy end of the branch.

The animal screamed a high yowl and caught hold of the stick in its teeth. With a powerful crunch, shredded the branch in its jaws. Tayen stopped and glanced down at the frayed snarl that was leftover, his eyes growing wide. It was no use anymore. He threw the branch away and the animal stalked toward him, snarling. Tayen backed away, glancing briefly around for anything to defend himself with.

I grit my teeth and smashed my foot into its solid, protruding ribcage. It yipped momentarily then turned and opened it's big jaws and screeched at me- a high, unnatural, spine chilling sound.

I squeezed my eyes shut and slapped my hands over my ears, expecting to feel the sharp teeth rip into me, but they never came. I heard a loud crack and the animal's voice cut off suddenly, then a thud.

I peeked out from between my lashes to see the animal lying, dead on the ground, with blood glistening on its snout flowing from the bullet hole just right and above its left eye.

I was breathing heavily. "So, Tayen... If you ever considered getting a pet..."

He gave me a dry glare. "I'm a cat person."

Suddenly Aaron's face was close to mine, his wide brown eyes shimmering in the pale moonlight. The woods were quieter than before- then Aaron started to talk. Stammering, and relentlessly running his mouth.

"I'm sorry Sirenna! I'm sorry," Aaron was saying, "I should have gone faster! I'm sorry, I grabbed your gun and I was gonna shoot it, but I didn't really know how and you were there then Tayen was and I didn't want to hurt you and-"

"It's okay, Aaron! Stop- Please! Please, shut up." My head was pounding from my own screaming and Aaron was making it worse. Aaron bit down on his lips and hugged me. His hand slapped over one of the slices the animal had left on my back, fiery and painful.

"Ahh! Ahh! Aaron!" I pushed him away a bit. He looked at me, clearly upset. I grinned out of one corner of my mouth and said, "It was a good shot, kiddo." He laughed nervously and stepped off me, but froze a second later. He looked down at his hands and they were glistening darkly in the moonlight.

I stood up, wincing and moaning at the painful stinging.

Aaron swallowed, with a struggle, then bent down and wiped his hands off on the moss, "Taaaayyen?" He called.

"I'm right here." His voice said, coming from beside me. I turned to face him and assessed his injuries.

He was cradling his right arm- I reached over and gently took his wrist. I pulled his arm toward me, the inside of his elbow an halfway down his forearm was wet with blood.

He pulled his arm away from me. "It's just scratches, I can wrap them up and it'll be fine... Jeeze, look at you."

The only things that worried me were the slices on my back. And my head was sore and bleeding from when it hit the tree. I felt the warm, wet, tender spot on the back of my head and decided I would live. I lifted my shirt a bit to look down at angry, red welts across my stomach from when the monster kicked me into the tree.

"I'll live-" I started, turning so neither of the guys could see my back. "What happened to your revolver-" I asked, eyes widening at the crushed, mess of bent gears and broken bits of brass and splinters of wood.

"The thing crushed it when it landed on me." He muttered angrily, unhooking the holster from his belt. "They make these so freaking delicate." He whispered a swear and shook his head, then dropped the mangled mess to the ground and kicked it away. He looked at me, noticed the blood.

"Let me see," Tayen stepped toward me and tried to gently spin me around but I held my ground. He tried to get behind me but I stepped in front of him- I was just being stubborn, now. He stared at me and sighed. I turned around wordlessly, obediently, crossing my arms and glaring at a tree.

I felt his fingers brush against my skin as he pulled the back of my shirt up to get a good look at my wounds. It made me shiver.

Or, actually, I think maybe it was just that the air was just cold...

Ugh, puke... I have become the girl I always wanted to punch in her stupid, boy-crazy, pretty little idiotic face.

# Chapter 18

"Okay." Tayen said, sounding professional. "It's not so... I mean, when you think about it..."

"Cut to the chase, doc, am I gonna die?" I tried to grin, but I was actually in a surprising amount of pain.

"No," He hesitated and then said, "But- this is... bad."

"What's bad? Who got hurt?" Lanné's voice came from behind me. I turned to see her walking toward us, trailing Kayleen behind her. Kayleen's face was as white as a ghost. Tayen nodded at me.

Kayleen stared at me looking worried.

"Are you hurt, Sirenna!?" Kayleen asked, in a high pitched voice.

"No, I'm alright, Kayl-"

"Oh my gosh!" Lanné cried "Sirenna, your back it's, like, soaked in blood-" I twirled and backed to the outskirts of the circle.

"Could everyone just back off? Jeeze, it's over... Let's all just cool our jets. Please."

I felt the tension around me loosen

slightly as a minute of calm settled over us. Eyes blinked and shrank back to normal size and muscles relaxed and breathing patterns began to regulate. Tayen watched me, concerned, the entire time. He opened his mouth to speak, I interrupted.

"Everyone just calmly... Have a seat, and relax a minute, 'kay?"

Tayen, Lanné, Kayleen and Aaron sat down in a cluster together. I glanced at Tayen who pulled one of our bags into the middle of the clump and removed a thin blanket. He whipped a knife out of his boot and started cutting part of the blanket into strips.

"There," he sighed when he finished.

He pulled out a container of water and wet a wad of the leftover material. He cleaned the blood and dirt off his arm, and wound one of the strips tightly around the cut.

We sat and watched, glossy-eyed

and tired. When he was done he looked across the bag in the center of us at me. "Now you- c'm'ere."

I blinked, dizzy, realizing what he meant and shook my head, "No I'm alright, I-"

"You haven't seen it." He said, pointing out the fact that I actually had no idea whether it was bad or not. I scowled and everyone shuffled around until I was sitting with my back to Tayen. "Aaron, could you hold this, please?"

"Yeah." Aaron wiggled over and held up the back of my shirt up while Tayen started to clean out my scratches. It was stinging really bad. I pulled away from him which made it hurt worse.

"Ow!" I hissed.

"Well, hold still!" He said, pulling me back by my shoulders. "You've got bark and dirt and crap like that in it and I have to get it out or it'll get worse, so don't move." He finished quietly, concentrating.

Kayleen looked up at Tayen, eyes big in the icy light. "Tayen... You said a bad word, Tayen." She whispered.

He flicked a glance at her and smiled. "Sorry, Kaylee."

Lanné pulled Kayleen onto her lap.

I sat still and put my chin in my hand, growling and complaining every chance I got.

I have to admit, though, it took less time than I thought before he was wrapping the makeshift bandages around my middle, making me wince every time he pulled it tight.

I'm not sure if he was doing that on purpose or not.

"Done." He sighed. "Was that so horrible? You aren't collapsing, so-"

I got to my feet, "Thank you." I muttered.

Tayen smirked and put the cap back on the water canteen. He stuffed the makeshift bandages into Aaron's bag as everyone stood up, sleepily. When he finished, we all set off the way we were headed before. We think.

As we walked, I couldn't help but think about what other surprises awaited us. Hopefully none that would try to kill us anymore...

*Right. That's likely.*

# Chapter 19

Zerago led his search party through the streets. By now, the whole kingdom was scouring every nook and cranny, looking for the children **Protectors** and their princess.

Omen had placed a huge ransom on their heads- still attached to their bodies- he wanted to kill them himself.

*Our leader is obsessive in that way.* Zerago thought to himself with a secret smile.

They trekked their way down the streets, moving away from the castle.

*The one place. The one place people aren't looking will end up being where they are, I'm sure of it.*

They were coming closer to the looming, black tree line. The ground was getting softer; the air was dusted with a light fog.

His men hesitated at the trees.

"What do you think you are doing?" Zerago turned around.

"Sir, that's- it's- the woods, sir, we- they're crawling with all sorts of horrible creatures, sir-"

"I don't care if the woods are crawling with swarms of winged insects the size of horses, with fangs the length of your forearm," Zerago glared at his men, "you cowards are going to walk in these woods with our Leader's anthem on your minds and your lips. "Even with our dying breath, we will declare the triumph of the Evermighty Overlord"." Zerago quoted. "Is this how you were raised? Sons of the Overlord. You dare to boast your allegiance when in reality- when finally faced with a battle, you bow out? Cowards. Unworthy Spawn of the Vanquished. That's all you are?"

The young man's pale face flinched in the bright white night. "No. Sir."

"March." Zerago commanded.

And they did.

They followed the orders as they had been conditioned to do.

*What had I been thinking? I am shameful. Dirty. Scum.* The young man thought, jaw set. *I hope I do die out here tonight in this forest. Better that then face the humility, the unbearable shame when word gets out of my sin. Forgive me, merciful Overlord.*

# Chapter 20

The Queen's anxious footsteps echoed off the dirty walls. She held her torch high and searched for any sign of her little girl.

She was so tired, but she had to keep running. It had only been a few hours since she had "died" but Omen would have noticed she was gone by now, and if he was as determined as before, he would have people searching for her already.

The Queen ran farther down the hall, her echoes ringing in her ears, and groaned as she caught sight of another intersection. She hated intersections; they made her feel like one wrong decision would take her farther away from her baby.

She stopped in the middle of one intersection and looked down each of the halls. All of them were the exact same.

She couldn't think anymore, her echoes and heartbeat were clogging up her mind. Now, she fell to her knees, tears in her eyes. She couldn't give up, but Brystone's Passage was so confusing!

Opening her eyes again, she caught sight of something dark on the ground where her torchlight didn't quite reach. She crawled slowly toward it and peered as the space got brighter. It was... a...

A bag, an empty bag. It was familiar, but where had she seen it-

She remembered with a gasp.

It was the bag that Sirenna had been carrying! The bag that was filled with emergency supplies! Each one of them had one-

That meant she was on the right trail!

But The Queen froze with panic. If she was on the right track now, then how was she to know which way to go from here? One wrong turn and she would be lost.

The worst way to track someone down was through Brystone's Passage. But at least if she surfaced now she would be somewhere near them. She decided quickly and got to her feet.

She ran into the tunnel straight ahead of the one she'd emerged from and took the first turn. She sprinted through the tunnel to the stairs and dashed up them.

She wasn't paying attention and almost ran into the wooden trapdoor, and, thrown off balance, lost her torch down the stairs. She watched as its orange glow bounced away and snuffed out somewhere below her. The Queen turned back and grabbed onto the handle of the door.

The Queen pushed hard. The door was heavy on the top so she pushed harder. Sand fell in, on her face. She shut her eyes and spit it out of her mouth and kept pushing. As the trapdoor opened, it got easier to move. She crawled out and closed the trapdoor.

The Queen looked around. She was on a beach, and it had been the sand had made the door hard to open.

She was on the outside of Scarandia, on the beach that surrounded the island. The cliff was reaching out over the water for thousands of feet. She shook her head and covered the door over again with sand and fell to her knees, breathing hard.

Surveying the sand, she noticed there were no distinct footprints left by the **Protectors** or Kayleen. No trail.

She closed her eyes as they started to prick, and lay on her back. The next thing she knew, she was dreaming.

# Chapter 21

After that last attack, we had been wary for the rest of our journey through the forest. Every rustle sent my heart racing.

Shadows seemed to make up silhouettes of fierce creatures. The ground kept moving and rolling beneath us. I was just hoping that we'd make it out before we got swallowed up by a Deiworm. *Yealch...*

We did get out eventually- without running into any more creatures that wanted to eat us. And were now resting on the outskirts of the forest.

Yes, there is a visible line where the forest ends. A distinct line where the flat moss turns to tall, gold and green grass.

I felt the immediate and immense lift of pressure from my body the moment I stepped onto the regular-feeling grass and off of that strangely squishy-mossy ground.

That whole time we'd been walking on that stuff I felt like we'd take one step and suddenly we'd just keep sinking into it and get swallowed by some mushy pit of carnivorous death-moss.

Mushy pit of carnivorous death-moss. Hoo-boy... that sounds dreadfully frightening doesn't it.

Attack of the angry woodland

bryophyte...

I'm *paranoid*, okay?! I tend to *be* that way sometimes to the point where, yes, I will suspect plants of being out to get us. Which has happened to me before, might I add.

Long story.

But anyhow, there we were, with the non-threatening-looking grasses and I was up while the others slept, watching- and not doing a very good job of it.

My sight blurred and drifted black momentarily. My head jerked up and my eyes snapped open. *Stay awake!*

I peered around the open field, looking for anything out of place, any strange rustle, any sound other than the quiet "hush" of the slight breeze through the soft, nice grass.

I shook my head and let it fall into my hands. I stared at the ground and stretched my eyes wide, willing them to stay open, but as soon as I raised my head and let my hands drop, so did my eyelids. *Ugh! This is terrible, I need to watch properly or not at all.*

I tried once more, shaking my head again and adjusting my position. The soft, fur-like fan at the top of a weed tickled the back of my arm and I jumped sideways. I swiped my hand across where I'd been, pulling out a handful of grass along with the furry weed.

I looked at the grass in my clutched fist and let it fall back to the ground, frowning.

*Ugh, jeeze. Okay, okay. I'll let someone else take watch...*

I cast my eyes across the group and took in all the sleeping faces. Kayleen was curled in a tight ball against Aaron's back but she couldn't be on watch; we were watching her, if I let her watch herself that would just be counterproductive.

Lanné was sprawled on her back- comatose. Aaron looked...well he looked young... and tired.

Tayen.

I crawled over to Tayen, and curled up beside him.

*As soon as he moves, I'll steal his warm spot.* I plotted in my head. I nudged his shoulder with my forehead. Nothin'.

I reached out and shook Tayen's shoulder and I let it rest there, my arm was too tired to move.

"Tayen...Tayen." I whispered. Still nothing'. "Tie-*yennn*, wake up..."I groaned pushing on his arm again.

"Goway..." He rolled over and I slid in beside him again, into the warm spot I had coveted, and closed my eyes.

"Tayen, s'yur turn fer watch..." I mumbled incoherently.

"Ugh, fine," Tayen moaned and sat up. He yawned and stretched, "What time s'it?"

I was only barely aware that the comment was directed at me. "I don't know... almost noon maybe..." my thoughts drifted too far away to collect any more words to make another sentence.

"Noon!?"

I was pulled up out of the dark, warm fog of unconsciousness by the panic in his voice.

"Yeah, yeah. Shut up now," I frowned, "I'm trying to sleep..." I curled into a tighter ball, and settled in again, soaking up warmth from both Tayen and the sun.

"Sirenna- We need to leave. It's full daylight!"

"Why? What's wrong with that!?" I whispered. "Do you have something to tell me- are you a vampire-?"

"We can't stay here in the middle of this big field in broad daylight, Sirenna." When I didn't answer he put one hand on either side of me and leaned over me, "Sirenna, they'll find us." He whispered.

I groaned and sat up suddenly, almost cracking my head on Tayen's.

"Well, where d'you propose we go, then, Tayen?" I asked, grouchily.

"I dunno," he sighed, satisfied that I was now cooperating. He slowly pulled his hands back and stretched again, "in the same direction we were headed before," he yawned. Tayen pointed to the dead woods. "Opposite of that."

I sighed, wishing I had thought to wake him up sooner so that I could've slept.

"Alright." I sighed quietly. Then I smirked. "But you're waking up Lanné."

"Nooooooo!" He groaned over-dramatically as if he were falling off a cliff to his death.

Made my day.

# Chapter 22

Hours. Hours and *hours* of walking. Or it felt like it. Realistically, it'd only been maybe three and a half hours. But that's still a lot.

We trudged through the tall, yellow grass, the sun hot and bright. I wiped a bead of sweat from the nape of my neck and let my head fall back and I stared at the fluffy white clouds.

Okay, now? Now it was *way* too hot. I closed my eyes as a delightful breeze danced across my face.

"Sirenna!" Lanné hollered back at me. I sighed and started walking again. I was surprised that I caught up to the group- but they had just been standing there waiting for me.

Which made more sense.

"Okay, let's sit down. Just for a minute. My feet are killing me." I suggested, but I stayed standing. "Do we have a plan?" I muttered.

"We were hoping you knew our plan." Aaron sighed, sitting down on the grass, squinting up at me.

I scowled. Well, my plan was to curl up right here and sleep but apparently that *wasn't* the best strategy for keeping young princesses safe from their demonic uncles.

Go figure.

"Yoouuu gonna sit down?" Tayen asked.

"I would, but my knees are kind of locked like this... I think?" I frowned.

Lanné chopped the back of my knees and I kind of half fell, half caught myself, and then slowly lowered myself to my knees.

Lanné smirked. "Better-?"

"Thank you." I closed my eyes and fell sideways. "Okay, let's get off this plain and find some cover- where we can sleep." I smiled and opened my eyes to look up at them, dark silhouettes against the bright sky.

"Sirenna, is that all you're thinking about right now?" Lanné said loudly.

"What about Omen and how we'll

fight him and what about The Queen?"
Tayen pointed out. I sighed, feeling
weighted all over again.

"Y'know, you guys didn't pull an all-
nighter last night. For me, this whole thing's
just been one big, long, crappy day." I
sighed but pushed myself up anyway. Sitting
cross-legged, I glared at them. "Okay, here,
I'll... **Look** for The Queen. Will that make you
happy?"

"Pretty please and thank you." Aaron
said quietly.

"Okay." I sighed then I closed my
eyes and concentrated on The Queen.

My sight switched from the black
insides of my eyelids to a dark, slippery
image.

A dream- The Queen's dream.

Omen was holding The Queen's
crown in one hand and Kayleen in the other
and laughing darkly.

I opened my eyes looking up straight into the bright, searing sun. I gasped.

Brilliant move.

"What? What did you see?" Lanné asked immediately as I groaned and tried to rub the dark and colourful spots from my eyes.

"*Nothing*," I muttered, "The Queen's just having a bad dream, jeeze, calm down." I sighed and lowered my hands from my eyes. Everyone was sitting now, resting momentarily.

Tayen sighed. "So, The Queen is fine-"

*For now,* I added in my head.

He continued. "We still need to get rid of Omen. How can we do that?" Tayen mumbled quietly.

"Well, there's gotta be some other

people who don't like Omen an' want The Queen back- maybe they'd help us?" Aaron suggested.

"Those people are probably farmers and regular people who've never held a sword in their life. They're not gonna be any good if it comes to a fight." Lanné shot down Aaron's idea.

"Maybe we can sneak back and convince some of The Queen's guards- you know, the ones who are still on our side." Tayen said.

"Yeah. Let's go right *to* the twisted madman, that way he won't have to come to us." Lanné said sarcastically.

"Lane, if you're just gonna sit there and criticize us and not help, then shut up. Unless you have an idea, just shut it." Tayen muttered.

Kayleen sidled up next to me, clearly wanting to stay out of what was turning into an argument. After a pause, she climbed fully into my lap and wrapped her arms around her knees. I rested my chin on her head and hugged her.

"Is it my fault that all your ideas are stupid?" She countered.

"Maybe not all of them are exactly the greatest plans ever conjured up but do we see you having any mind-blowing epiphanies?" Tayen was getting louder.

"No! You know why? Because *nothing* will work! *We* can't *do anything*. How're *we* supposed to "save the world" all by ourselves?" Lanné had now also raised her volume to her "I'm-angry-and-this-is-my-point-and-don't-you-try-and-*tell*-me-I'm-wrong" setting. She noticed this and fell quiet again, but she was still just as livid. "It's impossible- we're all going to get killed." She looked at me then after a moment directed her gaze to the ground in front of her.

Lanné wasn't just arguing anymore, she was scared.

She kept getting quieter as she continued. "We can't make miracles. We aren't magic or powerful. We're just outcasts. And we're all gonna *die* as stupid, hopeful, thoughtless outsiders-"

"*Lanné...*" Tayen hissed then looked pointedly at Kayleen. Lanné's eyes flicked to Kayleen's face and then back to the ground.

It was silent for a few seconds as her words and our own fear tried to smother us. I squeezed Kayleen. She looked up at me, scared as well. I met her eyes and smiled.

"*That* is where Lanné is *wrong*." Lanné glared back up at me from across the circle. I kept talking to Kayleen. "We're not *magical* or *powerful*. But we some pretty fantastic tricks up our sleeves."

"Like fireworks?" She asked quietly, eyes lighting up a bit.

I nodded. "Kinda like fireworks, yup." She grinned. "Plus there are people who *do* love your mommy very much and they'd fight for her."

Now I looked up at the rest of my family. "Sure, maybe they're not fully trained assassins with a sword but they're also not just brainwashed zombie troopers. They'll have something Omen's men don't, they'll have a passion- something to fight for that's not just merely a pre-installed expectation. And *we* have something Omen doesn't have- we have us, we have each other."

I was too exhausted to keep this tiring conversation going so I changed the subject. "So let's stop being at each other's throats, here, hm? Now, we don't need to figure this out right this second, why don't we all just brainstorm while we get to our next resting place. We need a base- like a place to store up energy and plans, right? We'll sleep on it." I suggested calmly and looked at Tayen.

"Alright." Tayen nodded. "Sirenna's got a point. Sorry, Lane. I shouldn't have snapped at you like that. C'mon, guys, let's try to make it off this plain before night."

Everyone dragged themselves to their feet and we started off again, Kayleen taking my hand as we marched on. Lanné stalked ahead of me without a glance back.

# Chapter 23

My mind was *trying* to race and find solutions to all our problems but the sleep deprivation thing was compromising my ability to do that.

Somewhere in between all our footsteps, the sky faded and got darker and the stifling heat subsided.

I peered up at the black, inky sky
and all the pin-prick points of light, the stars.

We did need to find some place to
crash.

Again, I wondered where we were
but without any new hints or clues, there
was almost no way to discern.

All of a sudden everyone shouted
my name in a big glob of near simultaneous
proportions.

"What?" I asked. Their eyes were
wide with shock and concern. I felt sick.
"What."

"Sirenna, look, you just about
walked straight off the edge." Aaron pointed
to the ground, or lack thereof, a mere step
or two away from me.

My eyes got big as I took in the
rocky terrain that would have been my not-
so-fun, quick ride to the bottom of a big,
steep hill.

"Oh..."

Well, at least it wasn't a rabid dog/monkey/bull thing trying to slice me open and slurp up my innards.

Plus it wasn't a sheer drop, just an extremely steep hill lined with sharp rocks. It was climb-able and walk-able... just not trip-able. Otherwise, well, there'd be a big mess for someone to clean up later.

I inched away from the ledge and nearly into Lanné.

Peering across the small valley, I was relieved to see that the hill across from us looked softer. My eye followed the small brook that ran in between the hills, all the way to the right where there was a forest (with living, green, normal trees) and on my left, there was a cliff. The stream trickled from off the top of the rocks like a tiny waterfall.

"Thanks, guys." I murmured.

"Watch where you're walking?" Aaron suggested.

"Yeah, no kidding." I whispered.

"Let's go this way," Tayen pointed toward the waterfall and started walking along the ledge.

"Wait, wait, hold on." I mumbled, peering down into the valley. "Let's just cross to that hill." I jabbed my thumb in the direction of the hill on the opposite side of the stream. "We should just stay on course- one direction."

There was really no good reason to go across the valley but there was really no awesome reason not to, so I began picking my way down the rocks, knowing the others would follow after me.

I watched my feet and the rocks as I manoeuvred down the hill. We hadn't gone far down at all when I stepped onto a sturdy, flat surface.

I straightened up from my cautious, balanced crouch, surprised, and saw a deep, dark, small cave. It was carved far into the hill and completely hidden from anyone above. It was perfect!

"Hey! Look what I found!" I called to the others.

They all turned to look around at the cave.

"Wow, it's amazing how much more helpful you are when you pay attention to where you're walking." Lanné said, breaking the silence as if on cue with one of her trademark snide comments.

Her cynical narration of my life was starting to grate on my nerves.

I glared momentarily in her direction, then ducked into our little temporary home to clear it of crawly things or other creatures.

Aaron was the first to collapse on

the cold, dirt floor after I herded everyone inside. Followed moments after by me.

I shut my eyes and barely felt the hard dirt crash into my knees and my hands as I fell onto all fours then crawled to the far wall and curled up. I didn't even bother to pull a blanket out of my pack.

I heard some brief discussion about Lanné staying up this time, before entirely passing out.

# Chapter 24

Zerago was getting frustrated. He was tired of looking and finding nothing. It had been a day and no sign of them, not even a shred of evidence. He snarled and punched a tree, it quivered. The men cringed as Zerago's red face turned to them.

"Sir, do you want to turn back-"

"No! Didn't you hear, I can't go back, I'll kill myself before I go back. We'll all kill ourselves before we go back to the Overlord empty handed. Keep walking..."

He stalked off and the guards stood in one place. The trees all seemed to quiver as he passed them. Zerago grumbled internally, not noticing where he was headed.

"Keep walking you slimy dogs!" He hollered at the men, he could hear the sound of their smooth, black armour as they crept deeper into the forest. Zerago shook his head, *there has to be something, somewhere-*

With a sigh he started to walk again when his foot twisted and he caught himself quickly before he fell.

He glared at his men as they passed, daring them to speak or laugh. They didn't, they just passed quietly.

After they were far past him, he

looked down to see what had snared him and ran his hand over the uneven earth. *What is this-* he thought as he thumbed the sharp stone corner.

"Uh, Sir-" one shaky voice called from far ahead,

"What!?" Zerago called, still assessing the large, square stone. The moss surrounding was torn up in a perfect square. Disturbed from below, perhaps? Recently, too- that means the children were here- which means they should still be close by-

"You had better come look at this, Sir..." Called the voice. Zerago hesitated but stood up and walked to where the men were gathered.

He followed their gaze and almost jumped back in surprise. On the ground, partially submerged in the patchy mist, was a Gorette, its skinny, grotesque corpse half picked apart by other animals.

A dead animal, Zerago didn't

understand the commotion. So they'd found an example of the circle of life, what was the fuss about?

He knelt down and assessed their surroundings more carefully and saw the faint hints of a struggle. Moss torn, depressions in the ground. Blood, on a tree. He ran a hand across it. It was almost dry, congealed.

Perhaps they were finally on their trail.

"Sir,"

Zerago turned, a man presented him with a mess of shiny metal and bits of wood in a leather holster. A **Protector**'s revolver.

He grinned. A trail, they were indeed upon.

He pointed at the footsteps the **Protectors** had left in the ancient moss and mud. "We've got them." He whispered, the smile taking over his face.

As he rose, in his peripheral, he saw a small movement. Something big, and black.

He was just turning to look closer when a Gorette came screeching from the shadows and tackled one of his men, the man's scream cut off in a thick gurgle as the monster ripped at his back.

*"Go! Go! Move!"* Zerago shouted and all the men snapped out of the horrified freeze they had been in and scrambled away from the creature as it turned its attention to them.

The Gorette screeched a noise so terrible, it was like sharp razor blades all down Zerago's spine.

He dashed through the forest with his men in tow. The trees were quivering all around them and there was a nasty growling and squealing above them. A huge black mass of two fighting Gorettes smashed to the ground, snarling and screaming, in front of Zerago.

He skidded and swerved, narrowly avoiding running into the two beasts scrapping it out. He glanced back, watching the monsters fight and sprinted headlong into a tree.

He sat up and tried to focus as dark red blood slid down his face and into his mouth. Zerago recognized the tell-tale metallic, salty taste. He spit it out and shook his head, trying to eliminate the slight shimmer at the edges of his sight.

Zerago saw large black silhouettes walking closer, drawn toward him by the smell of his blood, screeching high sounds that pierced his eardrums.

He covered his ears and scrambled to his feet, stumbling forward. He was tripping and stumbling like a drunk.

His eyes were slipping in and out of focus. He felt a sharp pain as he twisted his ankle and watched in wonder as the dark ground rushed up at him.

A sharp stab and then he felt warm wetness spread from his stomach.

Zerago heaved himself over onto his back and pulled the sharp stick out from his middle.

He could hear sounds in his ears like someone speaking through a long tunnel.

He stopped and looked for the sound, recognizing blurry human shapes calling and motioning for him to get up and run. He stared at them, as long as he could, but soon, the darkness swept over him completely.

He laid his head back on the moss and his sight went black.

# Chapter 25

*Drip. Drip. Drip.*

The Queen's eyes fluttered open,
then she squinted as the sand and water
reflected sunlight at her. She looked around,
suddenly disoriented.

She glanced up and saw dew

running down the inverted mountainside, dripping like raindrops off the rock in various places. One drip was right above her head.

There was a little trickle that was leaking down the rocks. Following it to where it dripped off the rock, she cupped her hands and let the water pool up. She took a small taste.

*It's fresh! Or good enough.* She thought and collected some more to drink and wash her face.

After she had finished, she looked around, shielding her eyes from the sun's reflection off the sand and water, but there were no tell-tale signs of the time. She knew it was late afternoon from the orange light and the longer shadow that the island was casting.

She pushed herself off the ground and stretched, brushing sand from her dress. She paused, stroking the big, red, velvety skirt.

*I can't walk around like this.* She decided.

The Queen walked over to where the island burrowed into the sand and picked through the rocks, until she came across a small, sharp one. She dug the sharp side into the top, velvet layer of her skirts, cutting the seam holding it together. She pulled off the heavy fabric and tossed it on the sand beside her, then cut off the sleeves.

She cut and tore pieces away until she was left with the simplest of dresses, one that wouldn't garner too much attention.

She tossed the rock aside, satisfied and picked up the stray scraps of fabric, collected the little pieces of velvet and gold trim and buried them in a deep hole she made in the sand.

The Queen stood up and her stomach growled. She paused and felt another pang of hunger and realized how long she'd gone without food...

She walked along the beach, headed closer toward the lower levels of the island.

First thing on her mind, find dirt to smudge on her face so that she wouldn't look like The Queen, then look for villages- for food and shelter.

She messed up her hair as she walked along the sand, hoping she looked at least somewhat different.

# Chapter 26

Omen stared at the men kneeling in front of him. They were covered in blood and dirt and looked scared to death.

"You're sure that Zerago is dead?" He asked the men. They nodded, gravely. He slammed his fist on the table and took a breath, "A Gorette attack?" They nodded again, "In the dead woods?" Again, they said nothing but their eyes told the story.

Apparently the attack was quite horrendous and only these three men of the original twelve had survived.

Omen peered at them. The ghost of the memory returned to Brenzin's eyes and the other two shared the same expression. Omen entered Brenzin's memory and saw Zerago's death for himself. He ground his teeth.

The failure got what he deserved. In fact he got off easy as far as Omen was concerned.

He exhaled and returned to his own mind. It was silent. He errantly wondered if these men would ever speak again.

He leaned back against his new gold throne, "I suppose I'll have to send out the dogs and their trainer," he mused to himself. He turned back to the men, "as for you three..." he looked at them, shaking, young.

"Get out." Their faces broke out into weak smiles and they nodded and murmured "thank you" s . He sent them away with a lazy flick of his hand.

As they left, a guard came in. It was one of the clean-up crew. He ignored the man and turned his gaze to one his **Followers** standing by the throne room door. "You!" He said. The guard stepped forward.

"Sire?"

"Go get the trainer. Tell them to prepare the dogs for a hunt- I have a job for him." The guard nodded and stalked out of the room.

The clean-up crew man spoke up bravely.

"Sire, we have searched the whole castle and we couldn't find someone-"

"I don't care about missing people."

"But, your grace, your sister, she's-"

"The *Queen*- she's dead. That's how I became The King."

"No, sir she's-"

Omen flicked his hand and with a flash of fire and bright light, the man was gone and the smell of burning flesh was all that remained.

Omen took a breath and looked around. He was bored.

"Entertainment! Get me something!" One of the men behind him jumped and scurried out the door. "Ridiculous, worthless men." Omen muttered.

# Chapter 27

There was a dull ache in my shoulder.

My eyes opened slowly to the inside of the cave and I sat up with a moan. I had been lying on my side and on a rock- it had been jabbing into my arm. I massaged my shoulder, frowning deeply, but the ache didn't go away.

I looked around- everyone was still asleep except for Tayen who was...

Gone?

I stood up and took another look. Nope, he was definitely not in the cave.

I stepped to the mouth of the cave and shielded my eyes from the bright morning sun. I squinted down at the stream- which was also reflecting the harsh light- searching for the cause of a loud splashing sound.

Tayen was down at the stream. Splashing water on his face and shaking water out of his hair. But that's not the reason my mouth fell open and my stomach dropped-

He wasn't, well, wearing a shirt.

And... W...ow...

I wanted to say something-something cool, witty or sarcastic. But it seemed as though *all* the words I knew were just meaningless jumbles of letters and shapes, let alone all the cool, witty, sarcastic ones. I didn't quite know how to say... anything.

It hit me then just *how* much Tayen had changed. Last time I remember seeing him with his shirt off, we were maybe ten or eleven and I'd teased him about his skinny, bean-pole-boy body.

Well... um... he'd certainly remedied that.

Tayen turned and saw me. "Oh, hey."

He stood up and was suddenly in front of me.

Water was dripping from his hair and down his... chest. He was grinning at me with that smile that could make angels jealous.

He was so close to me I could feel the heat of his skin. My hands were fists, curled tightly behind my back. I was leaning backward slightly and blinking a lot. I shook my head.

"Wha- why..." I stuttered. "Where's... Um-"

Tayen put his arms around me, pulling me into him and leaned in close and- and!

My shoulder still hurt!

I stirred and opened my eyes and- for real this time- I saw the cave.

Jeeze, that's... embarrassing... to say the very least.

I groaned and sat up, I had a big impression on my arm from where I had been laying on a painful, sharp rock. I rubbed my shoulder and glanced around.

Everything was all the same as in my

dream: Tayen was gone and everyone else was asleep- in the exact same positions, too.

I stood up, starting to fold up my blanket mindlessly.

I paused and frowned and looked at the blanket. I didn't have a blanket before-

My thoughts were snagged from the blanket mystery when I heard the splashing noises coming from outside.

I inched closer to the opening and peered outside in the blinding light- the same light as my dream.

And down at the creek was... Tayen-

His back was to me and he was splashing water on his face and his shirt *was* in a pile on the grass beside him. I couldn't tear my eyes away and soon I found myself staring at him. At least this time I remembered to close my mouth.

Don't judge me.

He shook his hair and water drops went everywhere.

I flushed a hot, deep red and with great difficulty, I recalled how to implement basic motor functions. But just enough to mechanically turn around, I stared at the cave as if it were some unreachable goal or checkpoint.

Then I heard:

"Morning."

I froze and considered just walking away and pretending I hadn't heard, but I'd already stopped. I faced him again, spinning too fast this time. He bent down and scooped up his shirt.

"Hi... Tayen..." I said, kind of quietly.

He pulled his shirt over his head and I took the opportunity to spin on my heel and disappear inside the cave.

I sat down and crossed my arms on

my knees, biting my lip. Then I kind of gave up and fell back and stayed there, laying flat on my back, glaring at the stone and dirt above.

*Well, I don't see how the day could get any* better. I growled sarcastically in my head.

# Chapter 28

"Food's gone." Lanné sighed.

It was a few days after my whole "holy-crap-Tayen's-shirtless" fiasco. We'd been bouncing ideas back and forth for a while but nothing was ending well so far. Things seemed hopeless and now, for our food to have disappeared, "things" seemed like they had it out for us and "things" just wanted to be evil and cruel for fun and entertainment.

"What?" I jumped up and walked over to her.

"Mice." She grimaced.

"Awuh, *no*." I mumbled. Holes in the cloth wraps that had covered our waning stash argued *actually, yeah.*

Yeah, mice. *Damn!* I swore in my head.

I went through all the pockets of our remaining bag one more time, hoping some conveniently hidden food would appear out of thin air. But of course, reality doesn't fill empty bags. And it doesn't fill empty bellies, either.

"Who was on watch last?"

Silence. Then, "...uuuhm..." Aaron looked up at me. "I think it might have been when I was on. I thought I heard scratching but I didn't think it was right in the cave- I thought it was outside, so I went and looked and there was nothing. But the sound kept going just like *scritchy-scritchy-scritchy,*" He wrinkled his nose and put his hands to his face, making scratching movements with his fingers, pretending to be a mouse. Kayleen laughed. I didn't.

He sighed and dropped his hands, catching sight of my glare. "I'm sorry." He muttered. I rolled my eyes.

What was done was done.

I grabbed the pouch of money and tied it to my belt. I tossed the bag to the far corner and plopped myself down. "At least we still have water..." I nodded toward the stream outside.

My thoughts trailed off, thinking about this morning and my dream. I shook my head.

"But, we need food-" Lanné started.

"How about we look around a bit- see if there's a house nearby and loot it." Aaron suggested. I stared at him incredulously. "Ha. Kidding..." He crossed his arms on his knees and rested his chin on his arms and shut up.

"Yeah, sure- nothing else to do." I said quickly, getting up again and stepping over    Tayen's outstretched legs.

Aaron perked up. "What, loot a house?" He grinned, excitedly.

"No."

"Oh-"

"Look around. Just look for *something*." Everyone stood up, slowly, stretching and working out kinks. Over the past few days, I'd grown to miss my soft bed back at the castle more than I'd expected.

"Yeah. Yeah, Sirenna, that's a good idea- looting houses- what- I don't know why I said that-" he rambled then looked up at me through his eyelashes.

I grinned. "You're a little twerp-" I ruffled his hair and gave him a soft push past me toward the mouth of the cave.

We stepped out of the cave and carefully made our way down the unstable hillside. We reached the bottom and crossed the spring, Lanné, Aaron and Kayleen stopped to splash their faces and take drinks.

Tayen flashed a look at me out the corner of his eyes, a small smile tugged at his lips. I slipped on the wet rocks of the stream and accidentally bit my tongue. I cleared my throat and kept walking, so that no one'd see my eyes start to water.

I hate biting my tongue. It *hurts.*

As we were walking up the other hill which was yellow and mushy- spongy, I paused and the others stopped and looked back at me.

"Shh- d'you hear that?" I listened. Aaron tipped his head sideways, Tayen frowned and Lanné just continued to pull her fingers through Kayleen's messy, wild, curly hair, but I knew she was listening, too.

"Sheep?" Aaron guessed. "A farm?"

"Where there's a farm, there's gotta be people-" Tayen said.

"Where there's people, there's gotta be a town around!" I exclaimed, a grin spreading across my face.

"Well, let's go then." Lanné commanded after a pause, nudging Kayleen up the spongy hill.

We came to the crest soon- since this hill was smallish- and stared down on a little town, nestled in the rolling, green hills. Perfect little "quaint-small-town" scene, right there. I smiled and we ran down the slope towards the road that led to the cluster of squat buildings.

Only after we were well into the town did I realize that where there should have been chatting and laughing like "quaint-small-town-towns-people" usually did, there was no sound. No bustling people, no talking, no animal sounds or anything really.

Puzzling. Very puzzling.

# Chapter 29

Omen looked at the signs on his seven rocks.

He tallied up what his hand would be worth, considering the signs and the color of the stone. This gambling game was simple, but it became very interesting when the stakes were raised. Players drew polished stones from a bag and the stone was a certain color and had a symbol etched into it. The symbols and colors meant different things and were worth varying degrees of points depending on how they were played.

Omen considered his strategy for a moment, then made his decision. *It's not my life,* he thought.

"I'll bet his life," he said pointing to one of his men, "and three rubies," he pushed the bloody coloured, fist-sized jewels to the center of the board. His opponent took in the stakes and swallowed.

"My life at your service and my next son's service to you as a soldier," Omen grinned and was about to lay out his stones when the dogs came into the room.

They snarled and thrashed and drooled and left deep claw marks in his marble floor.

Where there was fur, it was matted and dirty and their eyes were a cloudy yellow. The dogs were the size of a large wolf and had canines the length of Omen's hand. A trainer blew a tiny silver instrument, and though no sound that Omen could hear was made, the animals silenced.

*Unimpressive...* Omen thought, raising his eyebrows, and turned on the Trainer.

"Trainer, next time you need to bring your mutts inside, do not allow them to scratch up my floors," Omen said, curtly. The trainer bowed.

"I'm terribly sorry, Your Grace, I'll get the dogs some "castle booties"" The trainer smiled, eyes wide. Omen narrowed his eyes dangerously.

Any sane person would have curled up on the ground before that sharp gaze, but this person, the trainer was far from sane. Widely known throughout the castle the trainer had lost his wits long ago and now had no concept of right or wrong. Which made him prefect for this highly controversial position of gore and "justice"

Omen's nostrils flared at knowing he couldn't kill the trainer- he needed him. Omen stepped delicately as he circled the wild dogs, assessing them.

"These mongrels are the worst of the worst, are they? Where are your "prize-hunters"?" Omen grimaced as he saw one particularly ugly, snaggle-toothed animal.

"These are my best hunters. My *babies*." His eyes bugged and suddenly laughed a loud, a chilling sound. "Sire, they were bred to be able to rip prey to shreds, not look pretty- and they sure don't look pretty, do they..." He said, smiling as one dog began gnawing its own leg.

"How do they track?" Omen asked.

"They don't have preferences," the Trainer said, "Sire, they're mongrels. They get the scent, track the prey and kill it. They eat their prey, if they don't get it, well then, they don't eat." He laughed loudly again.

"They're not lapdogs."

Omen sighed and considered **Lightrixing** the Trainer on the spot. *No,* he reminded himself, *someone had to control these creatures,* he glared at the ugly dogs.

Instead he tossed the Trainer one of Sirenna's cloaks that had been found in her old room. The dogs went wild as the scent drifted past their snouts, the Trainer blew his whistle again, and they were still.

"When can they start tracking?" Omen asked.

"As soon as you pay me, Majesty," the Trainer smiled. Omen grabbed the three rubies from his gambling game and tossed them to the Trainer.

"It's a start," Omen said, "half now and half when you get me those traitors's heads on a plate," The Trainer smiled.

"A silver platter, Sire... that is- if I can get them away from the dogs." the Trainer grinned but paused, "Sire, if I might ask- is there any leads we could start at? And what are we hunting?"

Omen sighed but he closed his eyes and started going through all his spy's minds, searching for recent sightings. There had been no sign of **The Protectors** or Kayleen in Drayenn, the town surrounding the castle, or small country villages close to the castle, like Mattray, Untee and Call.

But when he stared through the eyes of his spy in Foreway his muscles tightened and his nerves tingled- he saw them, making their way through the small field, into town. Omen smiled, greedily and snapped his eyes open, staring at the Trainer.

"Foreway, they're in Foreway. Get your dogs to Foreway and follow the scent," he nodded at Sirenna's the cloak, "and you should find them. They're criminals, they've betrayed me."

"Foreway?" The Trainer's face

matched the hungry, almost giddy excitement that had gripped Omen's bones. "That's closer than I thought! A few days, if they stay there, and we'll have them!"

"Leave now. I want them dead as soon as possible."

"Why so eager... who are these people?" The trainer asked.

"I've told you, they are traitors. Traitors you should be tracking right now." Omen growled menacingly.

Omen shook his head as the trainer left swiftly.

Omen turned to his men and gestured to the game, "clean this up-" Omen turned and walked back to his throne. As he sat, he saw one of the men cleaning up Omen's stones. He watched as the man read the signs on the stones and turn green.

Omen sighed and settled into his chair. He closed his eyes, going back to

Foreway. He watched as **The Protectors** walked into town and headed for the first store. Omen commanded his spy to follow the kids and he did. The spy sat down outside of the store and Omen waited for them to come out. He'd make sure he watched them as long as he could.

If the dogs caught them while they were in town, he wanted to see it.

# Chapter 30

"No, Kaylee, we're not getting cake!"
I whispered firmly as the baker passed me
the three fat loaves of bread we'd
purchased.

Kayleen's face dropped. I sighed and
decided to compromise.

We walked out of the bakery with a pie, three loaves of bread and a smile on Kayleen's face.

I looked down the streets. All the people's eyes were empty. No one said a thing, I'm not even kidding, not a single word was being spoken. Nobody even looked up as we passed. We could have set all the houses on fire and no one would care. It was perplexing- they acted as if they were all dead.

All dead. How do you take that lightly?

I shuddered.

The bakery had been our last stop. In all we had five flasks of water, a jar of milk, some cheese, a map and the baked stuff. We'd managed to get all that and still have over half our money left over.

That would have usually made me proud but right now it didn't. The reason we still had so much money, and I knew it, was because the storeowners of some places were too depressed to take our money. We tried, I swear! They just stared through us.

Only one person had actually paid real attention to us. An old man. A skinny, white-haired, wrinkly, old, old, *really* old man.

But that wasn't a good experience, either because he didn't speak, he just watched us. Not once but every time we came out of a place, he was sitting across the street, watching us. We never saw him really move but he was just there, watching, wherever we were.

And here's the real kicker that we didn't know about until we had to cross the street and walk right by him- his eyes were so clouded and white that I couldn't tell you if he had a pupil or not.

He was blind.

Or at least, he looked like he should be blind. But he watched us, staring, if he could, straight at me. And it was a piercing glare that made me want to shrivel up and die.

I shuddered again and pulled Kayleen faster toward the end of the road. It gave me goose-bumps and I wanted out of that ghost town before we could find out what happened.

We headed out of town and towards the yellowed, squishy hill. I watched the ground as it passed under my feet, ignoring the curious looks from the group. They wanted me to come up with a good reason for the dead-town, but I avoided their eyes, because...I had no explanation.

I lead the way, setting a brisk pace and I stalked up the hill without a word.

I wanted to get away from that town and back to our cave. Everywhere we went, the people seemed depressed in a major way, which made me uneasy.

*Maybe it was just that town,* I

reasoned, *I mean, maybe they were all having a bad day, or something happened a long time ago that makes everyone sad on the anniversary, or someone died today, or everyone's sick, or something!*

We started to jog down the hill towards the stream but I still couldn't shake the sick feeling in the pit of my stomach.

If Scarandia was back to normal, the people would all have smiled and talked to each other, but no one said a word unless we asked them a direct question. Even then, sometimes people didn't speak.

It gave me a horrible sinking feeling that Scarandia had undergone a revolution while we were underground.

I shook my head. *No, that would mean that The Queen either gave up her crown, which she would never do, or she was dead... but I **Saw** her dreams...*

"Sirenna! Where're you going? Come back!" I looked back and I had walked straight past our little cave.

"Oh, sorry, I was just thinking about...stuff" I ran back and hopped over the spring and clamoured over the rocks to the cave.

When I reached the cave, I sat down and unscrewed the cap on my canteen and took a swig.

I shoved the block of cheese and two loaves of the bread into my bag along with the rest of our money. Hopefully we'd be more careful this time, watching for mice.

Then we started a fire in the cave from some dry grass in the field above us and some flint, which I considered a huge success.

Tayen made a tiny fish jump out from the stream with his "controlling bodies" feature and we feasted on his fish and bread and milk.

It was good, surprisingly,

considering the cooks.

I guess eating flat bread and salted meat from our bags for the past I don't remember how long kind of added to our extreme appreciation of the meal.

How long had it been? How long had we been gone now? Only a week? No, maybe longer. It's hard to tell how much time we spent in Brystone's Passage, but it really hadn't been that long of a time.

"D'you know we've only been out for, like, just over a week?" I threw out, while everyone was chewing. I watched them calculate the days in their heads.

"I miss mommy," Kayleen whispered after she'd swallowed her bread.

*Uh-oh, this conversation has taken a wrong turn-*

"Kaylee, you'll be fine. And your mom will be fine-"

"What's it like. Living without a mommy *or* a daddy?" She asked me. The others gave me looks that screamed "you started it".

"Well," I began, hesitantly, "I don't know much about my mom. But I like to think she was a good person. And I heard my dad was one of the men that went to hunt down Omen. From what I remember and what I've been told, they were both alright, kind of boring- maybe." I frowned. "And I wish I could have known them. But I suppose, eventually, you live with it alright every day. It's still there- like a shadow, but, if you've got other people who love you..."

Kayleen nodded, accepting my answer.

She tipped her head so it was leaning on my shoulder. I put my arm around her and I rubbed her arm. She yawned.

"Mm-hm. I kind of know that already- I miss Daddy but I'm okay, sort of."

She sighed. "But I don't want Mommy to get hurt."

"Of course not." I nodded.

"Kayleen that won't happen." Tayen said, sounding torn up. Tayen, sounding torn up, that was not normal.

"But I know Uncle Omen wants to hurt her- and me-" She sat up.

Aaron glanced at me, question in his eyes.

"Who said that?" Tayen asked, narrowing his eyes. Now he was getting angry.

Jeeze, he was just brimming with *feelings* tonight- *where did that come from?*

"It doesn't matter, Tayen, because it won't happen, right?" Lanné said quickly.

"Well, it does, 'cause people can't just say crap like this and-"

"Tayen!" He looked at me. I sent him a "Shut up!" signal.

"You said a baaaad word again, Tayen." Kayleen whispered. He looked at her and couldn't help smiling.

"I'm sorry. I have to stop that, don't I." He said. I could tell his blood was still boiling just below the surface and at the moment the last thing he wanted to do was *stop* swearing.

"What Tayen meant to say is that he doesn't think anyone should be saying things that aren't true." I explained to Kayleen. "It's scary to say, especially to you and that it was stupid of whoever it was to say those things."

Kayleen nodded and closed her eyes, slipping back under my arm.

"But, Kaylee, just out of curiosity, who said that to you?" I asked quietly.

"No one said it to me." She said

quietly.

"Well, then why would you think that?" I prodded.

"I heard you and Tayen talking about it."

My facial expression must've been funny because Lanné snorted and milk almost came out of her nose. I looked at Tayen and he silently beat the heel of his hand on his forehead repeatedly. A moment passed and no one spoke, then Aaron said:

"Well, that backfired-" He said swallowing a grin. Then he turned his big brown eyes up at me, feigning innocence, "wasn't it stupid of you guys to say those things?" I let my head fall onto the stone wall behind me, wincing. Ugh, I guess I deserved it.

# Chapter 31

*It's funny how long it takes for the sun to set when you're wandering along an endless beach,* The Queen thought errantly. She had been walking for what seemed like an eternity and the sun was only just starting to dip into the now flaming, red water.

The Queen sat down on the still-hot

sand and wrapped her arms around her knees. She looked out at the waves and tried to fathom how much longer those waves had been at this beach then she had. A small smile danced across her lips, *At least I haven't been here as long as they have.*

Her smile slid off when she wondered if her little girl was watching the same waves from somewhere else. She leaned her head against the warm, solid rock of the island and closed her eyes.

Her stomach growled painfully, she winced but kept her eyes closed. She reasoned that the sooner she fell asleep, the sooner she'd forget her hunger. Her thoughts drifted off into dreams. She recognized the terrible dream that had haunted her the night after night since she'd left the castle.

Omen was taunting her, holding her crown in his right hand and her baby in his left. And he stood, as always, laughing and sneering at her while Kayleen screamed and fought against the evil grip. The Queen could do nothing to help, either. Every step that she took towards Omen moved her farther away.

She ventured another step in desperation, hoping it would make sense this time, and reached out to Kayleen. She was swept backwards again and Omen just cackled. Then he raised Kayleen above his head. She slipped- she was falling!

The Queen woke up with a jolt. Her heart was hammering, Omen's laugh echoed loudly in her ears. A tear slid down her cheek and she wiped it away with disgust, *it was just a dream!* She scolded herself, *a nightmare,* she corrected, her mental tone softer.

She shook her head and pushed the heel of her hand to her forehead, hoping to stamp out the dream.

It didn't work.

She had always woken up at that same part but it never ceased to upset her.

She shivered and looked up at the moon's luminous face, shining down at her. She tried to lie back down and get more sleep but the warmth that had cradled her before had leaked out of the sand and stone, leaving the place cold and uninviting.

The Queen stood and picked up her makeshift mantle and wrapped it around her shoulders. She took a few steps then looked back.

The waves were washing away her footprints. It looked strange, like she wasn't even putting a dent in her search for Kayleen.

She peered down the beach and, other than the pace where she slept, there was no trace that she had been here. It was like she had never been there, never walked all that way, never tried. She wasn't getting anywhere. She wasn't making progress.

Her mouth turned down at the corners.

This beach was a dead end. She needed off as soon as possible.

She started to sprint along the beach, leaving footprints that made no difference.

# Chapter 32

I smiled, relieved, and opened my eyes and blinked before looking up into Tayen's face.

"She's on a beach, looking for Kayleen. She's not giving up." I whispered, excited.

"Was there any signs to give away what beach she's on or... where she might be near?" He inquired.

"No, I don't think even *she* knows where she is, the cliff doesn't go up too high, though. She'll be close to civilization soon." Then I shook my head, letting my smile slide away, "she's...disappointed, I don't know how else to explain it-" Tayen glanced at me, confused. "She feels like she's getting nowhere- not making a difference in helping anyone..."

He nodded and took a bite of bread, looking back down at the dirt.

It'd been about twelve-or-so days now since we'd first slept in our little hide-a-cave. It was working out well so far but I was getting anxious.

We still hadn't come up with any genius plans or schemes to find The Queen *or* get the kingdom back from Omen.

The sooner we got moving the

better but we couldn't run in blind or we'd be squashed like bugs in no time at all.

Apparently, Omen had already had an impact as King. My thoughts strayed to the little town we'd been getting provisions from. It was still as silent and lifeless as before.

"What are you thinking about, right now?" Tayen asked after a moment of silence.

He picked up a small rock and threw it at the wall. It landed beside me with a dull thud. I picked it up and threw it back at him.

"The town. How dead they all seem." I said. "D'you think it's because Omen's The King?"

He mulled it over. "I dunno if they'd be that upset, Sirenna."

He tossed the rock back to me, I caught it and looked right at him.

"Wouldn't you?"

"That's different, Sirenna- *we* all would. It's Kayleen's mom."

"It's their Queen." I argued, "Besides, their replacement is Omen..." I pointed out and lobbed the rock high in the air and caught it.

"Yeah, I guess that's true." Tayen said. He watched the rock as I threw it in the air and caught it again. "Omen as The King is pretty depressing."

This time, I didn't throw it straight up, I passed it back to him... without wanting to-

"Hey!"

He smiled and tossed the rock to the side. I pulled my knees up and wrapped my arms around them.

"Well, I guess we should be depressed, then, too." He muttered.

"Isn't that what this is?" I asked.

He shrugged. "I guess. The whole ambiance of hopelessness around us constantly? The haunting shadow of uselessness. The feeling that we're nothing but pointless existences lost, stranded alone in a maze with no way out. Yeah... I guess I could consider myself depressed."

He brushed the crumbs off his hands then put them behind his head and looked at the ceiling of the cave.

"Is that actually what you feel like?"

He shrugged again.

"I thought that was just me. When Kayleen's awake, I can keep myself distracted by distracting her." I lowered my eyes to stare blankly at the ground. "But when I let myself think..."

I trailed off, not wanting to talk anymore.

"So, I suppose there's no denying it anymore. Omen's The King." Tayen muttered. "But not for long, right?"

"Well, unless you've come up with some spectacular miracle-making-power, I- I don't know. I don't know what we can do. Yet. No matter what, we can't stop trying, right? You'll never give up on me, right?" I asked, eyes wide, suddenly worried.

"No matter what." Tayen agreed with a crooked smile.

I smiled back, reassured, and yawned and closed my eyes, preparing to drift off.

In the distance, a small noise had my eyes opening again, I frowned. "What is that?" I looked at Tayen, who was frowning and listening as well.

"I don't know..." He narrowed his eyes.

Barking, howling. And it was getting

louder.

"Sounds like it's getting closer-" He started to wake up Lanné.

"Sounds angry, s'what it sounds like." I muttered, nudging Aaron's leg. They sat up, sleepy and annoyed but they jumped to their feet when they heard the barking and snarling.

*It* is *getting closer to us...* I thought, my heart pounding. I jumped up and ran out of our cave to look for the animals making the sounds. "Aaron- take Kayleen as far from here as you can!"

Aaron grabbed a bleary-eyed Kayleen by the hand and ran out of the cave, down the rocks toward the spongy hill.

I turned to Lanné and Tayen and muttered quickly. "We'll go to that big flat field above us- it sounds like that's where they're coming from." We started out and up the hill, moving as fast as we could over the loose rocks.

Tayen got onto the grass first and turned to look at me.

"Sirenna, whatever is coming, sounds like animals and we don't know if our powers work on animals- you should have taken Kayleen!" Tayen muttered as I stood up beside him.

"Yeah, Aaron could have helped us more than you-" Lanné added, swinging her legs up and standing beside me.

*Ugh, they're right. I hate being wrong-* "It's too late now. He's already gone."

"Well, get him back here!" Lanné glared at me.

"D'you think I'll be able to catch up with him, tell him to run back and he'll make it to you guys before those animals do?" I gestured to the huge, scary, scruffy wolf sized dogs that were pounding toward us from across the field. Then I did a double-take. "Hey- they're right there."

Lanné and Tayen looked and finally saw the ugly mutts.

"Oh..." Tayen whispered.

"Whoa! No way!" Lanné cried. "We can't fight off the castle's hunting dogs by ourselves! You know they eat what they hunt, right?"

"Thanks for that, Lanné, now shut up and try to **Scramble** their brains." I commanded.

# Chapter 33

Her eyes narrowed at me then she peered at one of the snarling animals and it collapsed and tumbled.

It twitched for a while, but then it got up and loped off, looking slightly drunk.

"Alright, your powers should work

on them I guess." I nodded, feeling slightly less sick to my stomach.

I pulled my gun out and aimed. I didn't want to kill them, I aimed and shot. My bullet would have been a complete miss but for the freak placement of one unfortunate dog's paw. It yipped and crumpled, tumbling along in pain.

*I'm sorry!* I apologized to the dog in my head and bit my lip. I didn't like this.

I feel like guns are cheap, unfair and the go-to weapon of cowards. I hate them.

I groaned and holstered the gun, making another one of my brilliant executive decisions. But if I was gonna fight, I was gonna fight fair.

"Hey- don't let the dogs get near me, okay?" I muttered to Tayen, "I'm gonna try and **Send** myself over there." He nodded.

Okay, the fact that I was using my power wasn't all that fair. Considering, though, the fact that the dogs had sharp teeth and claws and a lack of conscience and I had neither sharp teeth nor claws and a *severe* case of having a conscience, I figured it evened things out a bit.

I needed someone to watch my body when I left it, because if my body got, say, ripped to pieces, even when I was not in it, I'd still die.

And we don't want that to happen, because I'd be no good to anyone as a little pile of meat strips 'n' bits.

**Protector** flavour, yum...

Why am I constantly comparing us to animal chow lately?

I squeezed my eyes shut and nearly begged myself to **See** through the other human's mind.

My sight flashed from the insides of my eyelids to the exact thing I had seen before except flipped.

Now, I was watching through the trainer's eyes as he ran toward Tayen and Lanné and my body. It was just standing there, looking dazed and lifeless, Tayen standing protectively in front of it.

Tayen being protective. Imagine that.

I could almost taste the trainer's thoughts, they were filled with bloodlust and his vision was tinted red. I could feel his thoughts, but couldn't read them. His mind was jerky and unattached. Thoughts interrupting other thoughts, unrelated words flashing through his mind like lightning, faces of people I didn't know, names and sounds crashing and screaming in his skull.

Being in his head scared me, I needed out.

I pushed my **Sight** out of him and I was watching him run again. I glided after him.

I smiled and embraced this weird

sensation. I was weightless and I loved it. I half sprinted and half glided across the grass after the dogs.

If I had my way, this is how I would spend most of my time. I felt so graceful, and I expect if I jumped off an extremely high cliff in this state, it would feel pretty close to flying. But I couldn't, part of this is that when I get in my own body, my head feels like it's splitting in tiny little pieces. Not pleasant. And the longer I'm like this, the more painful the headache.

I noticed that I had caught up with the crazy man.

I shook my head. *Back to business,* I thought. We were getting uncomfortably close to my troop now and I was only a few strides away from the closest dog.

I jumped up again and slipped through the air, landing lightly on top of the dog's back. It screeched to a stop; it knew I was there. I put my arm under its jaw and squeezed, pulling back.

The dog flipped on its back, trying to crush me, but since I had no real body, I didn't feel a thing. I shoved it over so that it was on its belly. I jerked the dog's head sharply to the side. I heard a sick pop and it went limp.

I grimaced. I absolutely *hated* killing things. Even scary, blood-thirsty animals that are after my family and I.

I let the dog fall and jumped up and glided toward another dog, tackling it onto its side.

As I was dealing with this dog, the others met up with Tayen and Lanné. One of them jumped high in the air at Tayen, who grabbed it around the neck almost in an embrace and swung it around with the momentum from its jump and released it, sending it flying over the cliff. It had ripped the neck of Tayen's tunic and left a smear of saliva down Tayen's neck.

Tayen only had time to notice this and make a face before he faced another animal, poised to strike at me.

The dog who'd started running straight at my body screeched to a halt, leaving ragged skid marks in the grass. It stopped inches away from Tayen as he prepared to kick its face.

It staggered sideways and fell over, brain-drained by Lanné. Tayen let it go, focussing on another dog. It suddenly turned its rage upon a fellow canine and they began to fight, snarling and ripping at each other. Tayen controlling the one that was winning.

I glanced around and saw that almost all the dogs were being dealt with already, the trainer was just approaching- a wild and crazy look on his face.

He was running straight toward my body and Tayen. If he landed one good shove, Tayen would go toppling off the flat into our sharp-rock-lined valley.

I took off and landed directly in

front of the trainer but he stared right through me as he slowed his pace, creeping toward a distracted Tayen.

*Of course he can't see me- I'm invisible to him,* I rolled my eyes at myself. Sometimes I wish they could see me. Again, it's almost not fair for them to suddenly get taken out by something they can't see- can't be prepared for- but... I got over it quickly when he made an attempt to attack Tayen.

Tayen caught him and braced for the push, catching the trainer and then they were locked together, both trying to flip the other over the edge.

I ran up behind the trainer and kicked my foot against the back of his knee with enough force to pop his kneecap on the other side. He howled and fell to the ground, holding his leg.

Tayen regained his balance in time to be charged by another animal and he threw a skull smashing punch right at the dog's head under its ear. It yipped and swerved, crashing into another dog- sending them flying, they too tumbled over the end of the grassy flat.

The trainer stood up and, with a shriek of rage, staggered toward Lanné. She snatched his arm and pulled.

*No! No! No!* I thought, as Lanné swung him over the edge. I flew down after him so fast, there was almost no reaction time.

I know- why save a bad guy, right? Well, what can I say, call me a saint...

When I got to him, he had only collided with the rocks twice. Well, only seriously collided with them twice. I put my hand at the back of his scraped head and linked my other arm through his. He screamed as he felt my presence and struggled to get away from me.

I wondered what I must feel like to him- must be terribly strange- since his hands were going through me as if it was air but he knew something was holding him.

I slid down the rocky mountainside trying my best to control the fall so that at least he wasn't tumbling all hap-hazard-like and splitting his skull open.

When we got to the bottom, I grabbed his left wrist and put my right arm around his neck. I yanked his arm up his back and kept him on the ground until Tayen and Lanné were finished with the dogs.

Tayen must have gotten into the mind of the dog that was going crazy and attacking other dogs. I looked away, it was gruesome. I wrinkled my nose and gagged.

The man started to squirm and I realized my grip had loosened. I pulled his wrist up hard and pressed his face into the yellow grass of the spongy hill, my knee on the back of his neck.

I looked at the three on top of the hill. Lanné was concentrating on the last dog- the one Tayen had used to rip a few of its fellow dogs to shreds.

I grimaced again at the bits of fur and pieces and bodies that were lying everywhere.

*Tayen's power could be the scariest of all of our powers.* I admitted to myself...

It wasn't the first time I'd thought that.

Once the dogs were all gone, Tayen came rushing down the rocky hill to the man and Lanné went to find Aaron.

"You- the voices! Powers! You- the ghosts- the voices-" The man whispered crazily.

His dark and yellowing eyes bugged and he strained to see Tayen, who knelt down in front of him and stared angrily into his eyes.

The man was ripped out of my grip

and was laying flat on his back with his arms pinned beside him as Tayen's control kicked in.

The man tried to scream and yell but Tayen made his mouth stay shut.

Catching a glimpse of Tayen's face made me hope with all my strength that he would never look at me like that for as long as I lived. His eyes were wide and scary, unblinking, his gaze piercing. I shuddered to think what he would be like on the receiving side of that gaze.

I tore my eyes away from his face and my vision flashed from right beside Tayen to way up on top of the rocky hill.

I took a deep breath and balled my hands into tight fists, getting ready for the headache.

I felt the full intensity when it hit me like a boulder smashing into my head. I held the sides of my head trying to keep it from exploding. White stars burst in front of my eyes and I rolled over so I was face-down in the cool grass.

When the initial blow had run its course, I lowered my hands and bit my lip to keep from whimpering like a kid.

Lanné, Aaron and Kayleen loped over to me and Lanné offered to help me up.

*That's uncharacteristic...* I thought.

"I get those headaches, too." She explained shortly.

"Thanks." I said, "but I'm okay." I started walking slowly.

Lanné shook her head and grabbed a hold of my elbow "Don't pretend like your tough- I know you're exploding inside your skull."

*No way,* I thought. Actually, I only felt like someone had stabbed a metal rod through my brain during a thunder storm and every wave of pain was a lightning strike crackling through that metal rod in my cranium.

I frowned. Yeah, she was right.

"Alright, let's go see what this joker wants with us." I mumbled, leaning a bit on Lanné as we made our way down the rocks.

# Chapter 34

The Queen collapsed in the shade of the first tree off the beach, breathing hard. She had sprinted as far as she could, now her mouth felt sandy and her throat was like cotton. She smiled. At least she had made it off that beach.

She pushed herself up again with

shaky arms and stumbled forward. She was so hungry. Where was she going to go to get food and a place to stay?

She pushed her way through the branches of the thick forest and got whipped in the face a few times by stray branches. *So much for people recognising me...* She though bitterly as another branch snapped across her cheek.

She pushed a small tree out of her way and a small, round, hard thing landed near her foot. She looked down. *Apples!*

She glanced up at the tiny tree. It was over-burdened with little green apples. The Queen picked one off and bit into it. The sour juice that leaked into her mouth was so delicious that she finished the miniature apple in two more bites. She grabbed more and ate them all.

By the time she was done, the tree had less than half of what it started with and The Queen was sure she would never eat another apple again.

She stepped out and continued her difficult trek through the forest, going uphill the whole way. Mindlessly she pushed on, not realizing how long she was staggering along her unseen path until the sky had grown dark overhead.

Now, with the pale, thin light, it was getting difficult to see and she was tripping over rocks, sticks and roots. She had already ripped her dress twice.

She tripped again and pushed her arms out in front of her to catch her fall and her hands met a rough, sharp rock. Her knee was snagged by a pointed stick, too, as she landed in the dirt.

Gritting her teeth, she waited patiently through the moment it took for her nerves to transmit the signal of pain. In the moonlight, she could see blood reddening the shallow scrapes that shadowed the heels of her hands. And on her knee, red was staining the white fabric of her dress as well.

The Queen sighed and crawled over

to a nearby tree that was wide and knotted and sat beneath it, mindlessly.

The sound of barking off in the distance, and screaming, caught her attention. There was something going on somewhere close. Close but not close enough that she would want to move or investigate.

Those were her people- abandoned by their Queen.

She wondered what was happening but after a long while, the air was silent again.

The Queen let her head fall into her hands. The Queen could feel hot tears budding in her eyes. She raised her head and took a deep breath as the tears rolled down her face. She moved to wipe them away but they kept coming.

So instead of fighting it, she leaned against the tree and let the tears soak her face and neck. *Forget it, there's no one*

*around. What does it matter anyway? I don't
have a face to keep up anymore. I've failed...
as a queen... as a mother. I can't even find
my baby! I should have stayed with her...
Kayleen...*

She burst into loud sobs that
bubbled from deep in her chest.

*Where am I? What am I doing?
Where are you, Kaylee?* She thought from
behind her tears. When no answers
appeared, she surrendered to the hopeless
and empty feelings inside of her.

*Who am I trying to kid? I couldn't
run my kingdom or keep it safe, now I can't
save it. And my little girl...* Her thoughts
strayed to an image of her bouncy blond
curls and her smiling face- triggering a
whole new wave of sadness.

*I'm no queen. I've never been good
at pretending I was either.*

And crying on the ground under a
tree, she felt like anything but a queen.

Her crying slowly gave way to shudders and loud sniffs and soon, her dreams took over her and dragged her deeper into unconsciousness.

# Chapter 35

I finally made my way down the perilous hill. My incapacity to walk a straight line really didn't help me achieve the whole "making it down alive" goal. But Lanné did. And sooner or later, I made it to the bottom and was now trying to narrow my eyes and look tough on the outside while I was still being stabbed in the head from the inside.

The guy looked pretty shaken if anything. And, oh yeah, he looked ticked off, too.

"I knew you were real," The guy growled at us. "You demons- I can hear you all the time." He nodded and licked his lips and his head twitched as Tayen released his hold on the man's neck up. "I can- I can hear you. I knew you were real, they said I was crazy but I knew. But I didn't realize it was you I was hunting. Don't they know I can't kill you? Remember? I tried- remember? Remember? I tried to kill you. Didn't work-"

He broke off as the whole left side of his face jerked. Tayen had released his hold on the man's body completely and soon he was writhing, twitching and squirming on the ground. He stopped convulsing and sat up, shaking.

I gave Tayen a wary look, he glanced back, confusion in his eyes now.

"I knew. I can hear your voices. All the time- I hear you- I do." His eyes flicked around looking at us.

"We aren't voices- we're children." I said experimentally.

"Don't lie to me!" He shouted. "You have the powers of the supernatural! The ones who talk to me. They whisper-"

"We're **Protectors**, dimwit." Lanné said, narrowing her eyes.

He froze and licked his lips again. "...**Protectors**..."

"Yeah," I said with a "no-freaking-duh" tone, "so what were you doing tracking us like rabbits with your mutts?" I waved my hand at the "leftovers" of the dogs Tayen had ripped up. Kayleen realized what those bits must've been and turned green.

*Whoops...*

"I was summoned by The King- He never told me I was hunting the bloody **Protectors**!" His eyes were wild, his voice getting loud. I remembered **Seeing** through his crazy, blood-hungry eyes. I shivered.

"You honestly shouldn't be hunting anyone, creep!" Lanné yelled at him, disgusted.

"I track criminals that escape from custody-"

"We're not criminals!" Tayen interrupted.

"He said you were traitors! He said you betrayed him! He said- He did-" He yelled, licking his lips again and twitching.

"What were you tracking us for?" Aaron asked, warily.

"Does it matter?" He started to laugh. "I was tracking you for the same reason anyone is. You're breaths are numbered-" He laughed hysterically. Aaron backed up a step, he continued to cackle, his eyes were rolling back in his head.

"What's happening?" Kayleen asked, panicked.

"He's snapped..." Tayen said as the man's laugh died out. Tayen inched closer and knelt down next to him and grabbed the front of the man's shirt. "Why do you say we'll die?" Tayen asked, calmly.

"He wants her-" he looked at Kayleen, who hid behind me. "And anyone else who'll get in his way of being King." Tayen let him go and the man stood and grinned, turning to face me, "And he'll kill you all with or without your powers!"

He cackled and pushed Lanné backward so that he could stagger out from our circle. Lanné's hands clasped the back of my and Tayen's shirts just as we began to race after the man, fists ready and teeth clenched.

"Chill." She said as the man ran away, "not a big deal..."

I swallowed my pride and let him

slink up the yellow hill and disappear over it.

"What... was that?" Aaron asked quietly.

"A very screwed up man who didn't know what he was talking about." I muttered and took Kayleen's hand, her eyes were still wide and filled with fear.

"What did he mean "he'll kill you all"?" Kayleen looked up at me, her small face processing way too much. "He doesn't mean that people'll hurt you to get to me, right?"

"I told you- he's messed up. Like, he's way gone. He's-" I made a circular motion by the side of my head with my index finger. "Coo-coo!"

She giggled and I grinned back but once we started walking back to our cave again, I looked at Tayen and sent him a very distinct "that-was-disturbing" look. He looked ahead and nodded.

I could almost hear him say: "Yup..."

# Chapter 36

"...then I escaped!" the Trainer was laughing.

Omen could feel his real body shaking and the spy's body did the same. Which is what usually happens anytime Omen controls people. Omen could be anywhere but he could control certain people. He used these people as spies- he had some all over the island.

The spy grabbed the Trainer's face.

"Where did they go!?" He asked with fury that could only have come from Omen.

"I don't know," the Trainer grinned, shrugging his shoulders, "I left first!"

He broke into loud giggles again and Omen **Entered** his mind and went through his memories of the attack. He could find no evidence, himself, of where they had gone.

Omen **Left** the Trainer's mind and threw him on the ground, the man kept laughing.

The laughing was only silenced when Omen kicked the man's face and then crushed his skull. The Trainer lay still, blood seeping from his head and Omen returned to his regular sight.

Omen looked at his hands and saw that he had clenched his fists so hard, his nails had made his palms bleed. He growled and whipped around, headed for the door. His guards made a move to follow him but Omen turned on his heel and faced them.

"I don't need people everywhere I go! Let me be! And spread the word that anyone who disturbs me until I come back will be decapitated on the spot." Omen snarled. The guards backed away, nodding and bowing.

Omen stalked out of the room. As he stormed down the hallway, he fumed.

*I need to think, how can I destroy them. I need something cruel, something evil...* He closed his eyes and took a moment to calm his heartbeat, his breathing. He concentrated mildly on his steps, slowing them, stepping lightly, carefully.

*I'll break them apart from the inside...* He smiled. *Break their hearts, watch them hurt, watch them struggle to understand. Crush them.*

Omen ran his hand along the wall as he floated up the spiral staircase like a shadow, silent and cold, imagining their pain.

Omen moved silently through his bedroom door at the top of the stairs. A wide wooden door, decorated in spider-spun gold, a thinly wound pattern that reminded him of chaos. He shut and locked the door, a quiet whir of gears clicking as the lock inside engaged.

He leaned against the door and closed his eyes. He saw the face of Tayen, the oldest boy. He would use him. He'd seen his life. He had watched the boy throughout his life, took note of how he acted. More recently, saw the change in how he acted around Sirenna.

*Sirenna.*

Omen's eyes opened slowly at the memory of her, smiling. He felt the chill in his spine, the tingle in his fingers and the sensation scared him. The only thing that scared him.

He crossed the room slowly, gliding closer to the mirror. The giant gold encrusted mirror spanned the entire far wall, reflecting the glamorous scene that was Omen's new private quarters. Everything he had coveted from his sister since he was twenty-six when his parents died, when she had inherited the castle at twenty-eight.

He followed her darkly, venomous with envy. Quietly hating her, a shadow. That was what he had become. That was all he ever had been.

Now, a mere five years later, he had it all. Everything he had longed for was his.

Except one thing.

*Sirenna.*

For years, he had lived so close to her, all her life, and she never cared for him.

Didn't notice him, acknowledge him. She was always with Tayen. Laughing, playing, falling in love with him. Did no one else see it? Was he the only one who saw?

But he never spoke.

Omen, the shadow.

But not anymore.

He slid his fingers down the mirror and imagined he was raking claws down the face of his reflection. Shadows brushed beneath his eyes, his eyes that stared back at him, like black holes in space at the center of a cold marble face twisted in anger and pain.

What was it!? What was he missing!? He had everything she could ever want, he could give her anything her heart desired. Gold, diamonds, clothes, animals, *people*. He had **Created Spells** so that he could have anything he wanted, become so powerful there was no *way* anyone could ignore him or deny him. Even her.

He spun and walked to the fireplace, throwing a ball of flame into the grate. The flames jumped and danced, sending strange shadow out around the dark room.

He watched the shadows move on the walls, feeling sick.

Omen moved behind the chair in front of the fire and gripped the back. He stared into the flames for a moment before **Searching** for the Tayen's mind. His **Search** took him to a small dark cave. He could **See** the other **Protectors** sleeping by a small fire. All of them curled up around the oldest girl.

Omen **Watched** through the boy as he looked at the sleeping face of the oldest girl; the boy was memorizing her features: her hair, her freckles, her lips...

White-hot rage flared in Omen's chest. *Why?!*

He pulled out of the boy's mind and with a loud hiss he hurled the chair at the mirror. The glass smashed, cracks instantaneously spreading to reach across the whole plane in split second.

The fire inside him faded and he knelt on the ground, surrounded by all the possessions he could imagine and yet, he felt empty.

He stared at his reflection in the shattered mirror. Broken, brought to his knees by a sixteen year old girl.

He crawled to the mirror and touched a long, sharp shard. Numbly he picked it up, the thin piece of the whole, so beautiful but laced with danger. He pressed it to the palm of his other hand and sliced an "X" in it. He watched his blood pool in his hand, crimson and vulnerable after being safe inside his body for so long.

He squeezed his hand into a fist and watched the blood seep between his fingers and down his wrist. He loved it.

He looked up at his reflection and for a split second saw Tayen glaring down at him. Omen blinked and the boy was gone.

Omen made his decision then, he knew what he would do.

He stood up, eager to put his plan into motion but he knew that he would have to wait until the morning. The nightly torture that plagued him since **Creating** his **Spells** would soon engulf him and he would be unable to execute his plan fully and it was vital that Tayen not have a chance to explain himself in between.

Omen shut his eyes and braced himself for the torture that would ensue any moment. The torment that would distract him, save him, from the real agony that was dancing in his mind, the image of Tayen kissing Sirenna.

He ground his teeth and waited as patiently as he could.

# Chapter 37

You know that feeling you get sometimes, when you feel like you're being watched? The one that feels like cold water running down your spine- I had that feeling right now.

Even though I was asleep, I could tell.

In my dream, I spun around, hoping the feeling was a figment of my subconscious. But no one was behind me. Or at least not in my dream...

I was sure I was alone in this dream, but I still felt unseen eyes on me. I wandered a bit, searching for a stalker and peered around, looking for a sniper. Nothing. In fact there was not another living thing in this creepy little dream of mine. But the sensation was growing stronger and more adamant in its battle for my attention.

I dragged myself out of the depths of sleep and peeked through my eyelashes. The only person that I could see that was awake was Tayen.

I looked closer at his face and he *was* the one watching me. He was looking at me with an expression like...like... I don't know what. I couldn't read his expression well enough.

I yawned and moved my head and opened my eyes, blinking, pretending I had been asleep- as if I hadn't caught him watching me. I was stealthily taking in his expression, though.

It was almost... fascination? Adoration? He shifted his eyes- pretending to be watching the mouth of the cave, now. I frowned. Well, whatever the expression was, I can't put my finger on it.

That's going to bug me, now...

"Hey, why are you awake?" He asked me, faking, like he just noticed I had woken up.

"What, am I not allowed to wake up?"

He smiled a bit. "It's the middle of the night."

"I wanted to take watch." I lied.

"Yeah, just as much as I want to live *here* for the rest of my life," he grinned then narrowed his eyes, "you hate being on watch."

"No!" I raised my chin defiantly. "You don't know that, Maybe I just wanted you to get some rest."

"Go back to sleep. I got this, it's fine."

Since I wasn't really interested in taking watch- truthfully, I do hate it- I began to close my eyes. I was about to drift off when curiosity overwhelmed me.

"What were you thinking about while you were on watch just now?"

"What do you mean?" He eyed me suspiciously, now.

"Like, what do you think about when you've got no one to talk to."

Relief flashed across his face for a moment, then he thought and spoke. "I dunno, Omen, Kayleen, The Queen. Stuff like that, I guess."

*Ugh, yeah right, that's my excuse!*

"We all think about Omen and Kayleen and The Queen, Tayen. I meant what else?"

"Why do you care so much?" He looked wary, now. He thought this was strange, even for me.

"I'm curious..." I said, trying to stay as close to the truth as I could.

"I think about..." he sighed, "life... and stuff- go back to sleep."

"That's... I don't get it." I admitted, ignoring his earlier comment. "Why? What part?" That question did it.

"I... I want to know if there's more. Like, more than just protecting and training and running and fighting. I don't regret any of it, I mean I still know what I *have* to do... watch Kayleen, keep her safe, yadda yadda yadda. But at the same time... I have to know I'm worth more than that, y'know?"

"Oh." I said, digesting his sudden explanation.

"I mean," he sighed, "d'you remember when The Queen and King's **Protectors** were killed in that first battle? When The King was killed?"

"Yeah," I nodded, solemnly. How could any of us forget?

He continued. "Everyone felt bad for them but, they all focussed mainly on The King..." He shook his head. "Those **Protectors**... They were the best of the best. But no one really cared- I mean really, really cared. They had no friends and they're parents didn't even know them..." He paused, thinking.

That was probably the most I'd ever heard him say in one sitting.

"I wonder if my parents would care if I died..." He said suddenly. "If anyone would care..." He looked at the ground. I knew where he was coming from and I knew how lonely it could feel. I reached over and touched his hand.

"I would." I tried to comfort him. He pulled away, shaking his head and I frowned.

"I know, but you don't count. That's not what I mean. You don't get it..." my spine tingled and my cheeks burned as the rejection set in.

He kept talking, not noticing my expression.

"I feel like something's missing, like, life isn't really-" he searched for the right words. He looked at me and took in my face.

He paused. I could see him rerunning the last few seconds in his head, he glanced briefly at his hand and back at me. He closed his eyes when he realized what he'd said and he started to apologize.

"No, Sirenna, that's not what I mean-" he said again.

"Oh, it's fine- not like I know what you've been through or anything. Forget it." He opened his eyes and I glared straight at him. "'Cause I don't count. Right?" I let cold ice coat my words and he sighed.

"Sirenna-"

"Whatever."

He was silent after that.

I fumed for a while but after I cooled down, I rethought my *slight* over-reaction. I wasn't over it enough to talk to him again right now. But I knew I'd be begging for forgiveness tomorrow morning. It was a small slip and it wasn't intentional. I decided to just sleep and address it in the morning- that would probably be best.

*We'll talk in the morning, he'll forgive me. Right?*

# Chapter 38

When I woke up the next morning, Tayen wouldn't look at me. He wasn't acknowledging me when I spoke to him, when I asked him a question, even when I hovered right by him. Nothing. And it hurt.

But that was nothing compared to what happened later that morning.

Something inside him snapped and it was... the scariest thing I have *ever* encountered and to this day, my worst nightmare.

Aaron tried to make a joke, tried to break the tension that had been hovering over us all and Tayen spat a cruel insult at the eleven-year-old boy. I saw Aaron react as if the comment was a physical force. His body, taking a violent hit. His eyes wide, his mouth open. He started to cry but tried his best to hide it.

Tayen had never said anything cruel to Aaron. Aaron loved Tayen, adored him, probably more than he loved anyone else on the planet apart from Kayleen. Tayen was Aaron's big brother, he really was, and he would never say anything to hurt Aaron, ever.

Except just then and Aaron was destroyed.

Lanné, feeling obligated and being characteristically easily ignited, came to Aaron's defence and said one of her snide comments and that's all it took to set Tayen off entirely. He retorted with acid and then they were going at it. Lanné, with her hot temper and wide range of insults firing slicing words at Tayen, who I had suddenly become a stranger.

He and she fought often, but they never really truly meant to hurt one another.

Today was different. Tayen aimed for the kill. Lanné attacked back with a blinding hate, throwing every dirty, astounding, horrible insult at him that she had stored up. I started yelling over Lanné to shut her up and Lanné turned her rage on me.

Kayleen started to cry and soon she was in hysterics. It was when Tayen glared her way and yelled at her to shut up that everything went silent.

After a stunned second, Lanné launched herself at him, tackling him to the ground, scratching him across the face. It took less than a second for us to react. I wrapped my arms around Lanné's torso and tried to pull her away and Aaron tried unsuccessfully to put himself between them.

Tayen pushed Aaron away and was on his feet in a moment. In a movement so sudden even I didn't trace it, much less freaking *expect* it, he punched Lanné so hard it almost sent us both to the ground.

It shocked her into silence. Shocked us all into silence, but Lanné... she could *not* place what just happened. She had no reaction- it had never happened before. She wasn't sure how to take it. Her body didn't *know* how to react.

I let her go and tried to turn her around, tried to get her to look at me, but she wouldn't. She just stared open-mouthed as her eyes started to tear up. She would only stare over my shoulder at Tayen.

Remember, this is Lanné. She cries even less than I do, and even as Tayen stared back at her as tears slid down her cheeks, he stalked past us without a word and disappeared out of the cave.

She wouldn't talk for hours afterward. She sat inside, just biting her lip trying not to burst into full-out sobs, glaring at the ground. I tried talking to her but she would do nothing, ignoring me also. When I finally got her to speak, she was the most stinging and venomous that I'd ever heard her get.

Guilt consumed me. Was this *all* my fault? What had happened last night that made him like this- he would never, *never* treat us like this. I had never seen him treat *anyone* this way, let alone us. His family. He loved us, I knew he did. But today he wakes up and suddenly he wants us to die? I felt sick, terrible. This couldn't be all my fault.

And that is what sent me running out to the stream, holding myself over it, truly and completely ready to vomit. He wouldn't speak to me- would *not*. But I didn't care anymore.

He'd stepped *way* out of line. And

now he was going to pay.

# Chapter 39

I was shaking with fury as I made my way over to the thin, tall figure standing, arms crossed, with his back to me, in the fog that had settled over this day. Fittingly, like a shroud.

Tayen was staring into the mist as if he could set it on fire and burn us all alive.

I started out with pure, unmasked fury and a bunch of swears and curses that I don't think I can repeat. But it seemed all the swearwords and shouting in the world would not break his determination to ignore me.

"You wanna hurt someone, Tayen? Hurt me, hurt me all you need to but you cann*ot* take it out of the kids and expect me to take *that* quietly-"

He turned and faced me suddenly and he grasped my arm tightly. I gasped at the pain but partly at the drastic change in his features. His bright eyes were no longer warm and shining; they seemed remote and dull and his face was cold and reserved.

"You want me to *hurt* you? I can hurt you, Sirenna. You have no idea how badly I want to-"

"*Tayen*-" My eyes were swimming, his grip on my arm sending outrageous pain shooting through my whole body.

He started to walk, yanking me along behind him. He dragged me along the stream, toward the waterfall, to where the rock jutted almost straight up from under our feet. Then he turned sharply and pulled me up the rocky hill a ways until we were halfway up, away from the waterfall but the rock that slanted upward still went up another five feet above my head.

He slammed me against the rock and stared into my eyes with a fury that I had never imagined he could hold.

"You *want* me- to *hurt* you?" He hissed, putting his hands on either side of me so that I had no escape. "I can *do* that-" He set his jaw and I looked away. He grabbed my face and made me look at him.

He had blonde hair, green eyes, all the same freckles in all the same places on his face tanned from being in the sun, but this was not Tayen.

He released my face and pinned both my wrists against the rock behind me. I glared daggers at him- what point was he trying to prove with this.

With sudden resolve in his eyes, his gaze that was burning into mine, he swooped in and pressed his mouth to mine, violently, painfully.

I turned my head, shocked and then squirmed angrily and swore as loud as I could.

He looked up at me and covered my mouth, eyes boring into my soul. I clawed at his hand and his arm, leaving scratches. He dropped his hand and smiled "Hurt yet?" He asked as if what he had just done was *merely* a hard shove or a crushing punch or a knife in the back.

"...Tayen..." I was crying now. He let me go I fell to my knees and he turned from me and started to walk away.

"I'm going to the castle." He told me over his shoulder. "Whether you're coming or not. I'm done with this."

I knew what he meant by that. It could only mean one thing- suicide.

And at this point, I would not put it past him to actually follow through.

It was overwhelming and stifling, I was colder than before and I knew it had nothing to do with the temperature.

"Let's go!" I heard Tayen's voice call from somewhere hidden behind a curtain of fog. I stumbled to my feet and tripped after him in the direction of his voice.

I couldn't believe this. I couldn't... process it.

Yet another thing that Tayen had done today that didn't make sense.

Tayen... he'd...

But his eyes were so... dead. It wasn't him... It couldn't be. Something was way too wrong for it even to be Tayen...

I shuddered and pushed that thought out of my mind.

I steadied myself and took a deep breath, the wet air smelled fresh and I imagined exhaling everything that had just happened. It didn't work. I took off after him again.

I didn't even glance at the three other scared, angry faces, my focus was on Tayen. He had already started to walk away, Lanné, Aaron and Kayleen had stayed back to wait for me.

I jogged to catch up with Tayen and pulled his shoulder back. He barely moved. He just stopped and stared at me, angrily.

"Tayen! Tell me! What the hell is going *on*?" He turned away again, continuing on. "Whatever it is- I- you can *tell* me!" I called after him, tears in my eyes again. He didn't look back.

"I'm getting to the castle as soon as possible." He said in a strange tone.

"Why? *Why*?! When was this decided?"

"Last night. I decided that we are going back to the castle." He said quietly.

"We can't go back! What about Omen?" There was something really wrong here. He didn't look like himself, sound like himself, he wasn't thinking straight... was all of this *really* my fault?

"Omen isn't a threat."

"What? Of course Omen is a threat! He could kill us all!" He ignored me and continued walking robotically along the rocky hill. "Tayen- listen to me!" He didn't. "Stop walking!" I yelled and gave a hard heave on his arm, he didn't stumble or even step back like a normal person would have. He sighed and turned to me.

"What if I don't care anymore, Sirenna? What if I don't want to live with this- with you? Maybe you don't matter." *You don't count...* He smiled but it wasn't a reassuring, nice one- it scared me.

"What?" I whispered. I was broken, now. Ripped in half. "You're not serious." My sight blurred from behind the tears in my eyes. I blinked and some more fell out.

"If you're coming along, then just follow me and keep your mouth shut." He turned from me and walked on.

A moment later, Lanné appeared behind me.

"Let him go. Let him kill himself." She stared at his back, arms crossed.

"What?" I shook my head.

"If he's going to be like this- if he's going to do this-" she pointed angrily at the bruise that was appearing under her left eye, "let him go. Or I'll kill him myself."

"No!" I was appalled. "I know he hit you, he's hurt us- in ways he has never even come *close* to hurting us ever before- I've known him all my *life."* I stared after him. He had stopped walking. "But this isn't him. I would say let him kill himself, too. If I wasn't sure that my Tayen is still in there somewhere." I stared deep into Lanné's eyes, holding her gaze with a determination that I couldn't explain.

Her eyes started tearing up again as I watched her. She squeezed her eyes shut and looked away, trying not to burst into violent sobs. Her hands were covering her face and she started to cry. I pulled her into a tight hug and I felt her nodding, gasping in breaths and then she stepped back and lowered her hands.

She set her jaw and looked up at me, eyes still streaming.

"Let's go." She said, now just as determined as me.

# Chapter 40

Anastasia wiped her brow and looked far ahead, she still had so much more to-

She peered through the leaves, there was light. It was grey and dull but it was foggy outside today. She shivered as she remembered sleeping outside in the cold last night. She was exhausted but at least there was a small stream running past her in case she got thirsty.

She began toward the thinning trees but ended up moving into the brook, where there were fewer trees to snap her in the face. The rocks were slippery but she made it without falling and knocking herself unconscious. She broke through the last few bushes and glanced around.

There was nothing, if she followed the stream, she'd run into a rock wall. And on either side of her were hills, one rocky and one yellowed. And now her feet were cold. She put her hand on her forehead and closed her eyes. She was about to cry again when she heard a tiny, far away "whoa!"

Her eyes snapped open and she frantically searched for the voice. Her heart leapt out of her chest. There were five children-sized people just cresting the grassy hill, one had slipped but whomever was holding the small child's hand had pulled her back up.

"Hey!" She yelled. She splashed through the water and ran at the spongy, yellow hill. She scrambled her way up as fast as she could, considering the slippery conditions. "Hey! Wait!"

Did she dare hope for such an impossible idea? What were the chances?

She dashed up the hill anyways, people were people. And she needed to speak to a person.

But did those kids ever look similar- *No, don't get your hopes up!*

She ran harder anyways.

"Stop! Hey!" she yelled as she came to the top of the hill, the kids turned to face her. Her eyes were drawn to the smallest one with Anastasia's own, violet eyes.

*Kayleen... Oh, God! It's her!*

The little girl's smile was dazzling and just as she remembered. Tears leapt from her eyes and she sprinted full out down the hill. Her baby ripped out of Sirenna's grasp and ran as fast as her legs would allow.

The Queen held her arms out and fell to her knees. Kayleen smashed into her, crying.

# Chapter 41

We caught up to him quickly, and though I still hadn't caught my breath from Tayen's verbal and emotional punches to my gut, I was prepared to try my best to save him.

But I felt that this was bigger than me. His cold, dead eyes, his cutting words, that painful kiss.

I wanted to forget that the most out of the whole thing. That *was* a hurt that was more painful than any word he could have ever said to me.

"Woah!" Kayleen slipped and I hauled her back up without a word.

I walked in silence. We all walked in silence, actually. The ground had levelled out and we were going in a direction that was unfamiliar. I didn't care. I would just follow, for now and ask questions when my brain was a little more aware.

Speaking of aware, I heard a small cry from behind us. I did a quick head count. Everyone was here-

"Stop! Hey!" The voice called from the hill. Kayleen froze.

"I know who that is..." she whispered. We all turned around.

It was her.

*How had she found us? Why was she here? I didn't know she was so close, or I would've-*

Kayleen tore away from me and booked it to The Queen. Tayen cursed behind me.

"No! That's not possible!" I stared at him.

"What do you mean "not possible"? You knew she was alive! I told you, remember?" I stared at him, disbelieving.

He paid no attention to me, but stared on toward the Queen with that same hate that made my soul shrink. I ripped my eyes away from his face but before I could say anything, I was swallowed into a tight hug. Tayen watched, silently.

"Sirenna! Thank you so much!" The Queen said, smiling.

"It's my job..." I mumbled into her shoulder, still partially numb.

"I will forever owe you! So much!" I shook my head.

"You don't owe me anything." She looked back down at Kayleen and held her tightly again. "I mean, it's my job."

The Queen moved to embrace Tayen but he backed away as if the Queens arms were red hot. "Thanks is more than enough." He forced out. And turned on his heel

"Tayen-" I started.

"What are you doing?" The Queen demanded him.

"We are going to fight Omen." He said evenly.

"You can't fight him, what are you thinking!?" The Queen's eyes grew wide. "My entire kingdom couldn't do it. You can't do it alone."

"You are welcome to join the cause. Whether you do or not I've decided we are going to the castle."

"I can't allow you to do that."

"You can't stop me."

"Tayen-" I began.

"Shut up." He didn't even glance at me.

Another good slap in the face. The Queen seemed at a loss for words.

He continued, undeterred. "You are no longer The Queen. Therefore you have no more power over me or anyone." He turned and continued to walk to the castle.

Again, the waves of nausea. I tried to swallow it away but my throat was debating on whether I should do that or vomit.

"He's not himself- we don't know what's wrong." Lanné explained darkly.

"Then why are you following him?" The Queen asked, appalled. I was too embarrassed to answer.

"So he doesn't kill himself." Aaron said quietly. "He's part of our family, we're all we have. Us 'n Kayleen, I mean."

"Well, I am thankful that you watched my daughter, but I will not let her anywhere near Omen ever again."

I wanted to say something but all I could do was stare at the grass.

"No! She *must* come!" Tayen said suddenly. Nobody spoke. "I- couldn't bear to be apart from her- right now." He said robotically.

"Alright, but we are not going to the castle." The Queen said as if she was testing cold water.

"As long as she's near enough-" Started Tayen.

"Near enough for what?" I asked, quietly, looking up from the ground.

"Wouldn't you like to know." He muttered under his breath.

I felt like crying.

# Chapter 42

Days of this. Days of this evil, cruel Tayen that nobody could reach. Nobody could get anywhere with him, not even The Queen. Her least of all of us, in fact.

I was afraid to go anywhere alone with him as he was. Lanné noticed this and asked me why. I just shook my head and told her I couldn't explain it, it was just a feeling.

Truthfully, though, it was fully explainable.

I never wanted to give him a chance to ever hurt me the way he had by the waterfall ever again.

The strangest part was that through the nights, Tayen convulsed the entire time-without breaks or pauses. His mouth was jammed shut, though he was screaming in his sleep. He would sit up and grab at us, whoever was closest and try desperately to say something but it was as if he had lost control of himself and was struggling to gain control back again. He fought endlessly through the nights. His eyes would not open from the instant he closed them until the moment he sat up, cold and angry all over again.

Except once. One time, his eyes and mouth snapped open at the same time and he bolted upright. His eyes wheeled, searching for me, he grabbed me and pulled my close and said:

"O- Omen! He's- he's inside- get away-"

His eyes rolled back and his jaw cemented shut and Tayen cried out, angrily until he fell backwards once again. I was sobbing.

Now it was almost sunset on the third day of straight, merciless marching back toward the castle and we were creeping along the stone wall that surrounded it.

"Listen. Tayen, this is madness, you said it yourself- Omen is inside the castle we've got to get away from here-" he smirked but kept walking. I continued, pulling at his shirt. "If we leave now, we can get out before anyone notices us-"

"No. Our only chance left is to go this second while his men are switching watch. It's a ten minute window and we've got to go now or we'll get caught. It's our only option."

I searched his face for any sign that this was a sick joke.

"No, it's not, we have another option, I call it the "get-the-hell-out-of-here" option. Otherwise known as the sane option!" He took off without acknowledging me.

I ran my hand over my face and Kayleen patted my arm.

"He can't just-" I started.

"Let's go." He pulled at my arm, roughly. I yanked his face close to mine.

"Are you insane? Have you lost your *mind*? Omen will *kill* us. We will *die*, Tayen. How is that escaping you!?" I said. My voice quivered and my hands were shaking.

"We need to finish this. I want it done now. Besides if we wait too long, they'll all be back." He ripped his arm out of my hand and slipped across the large castle grounds.

"C'mon, we can't let him kill himself." My voice cracked at the last two words. I crept to the castle wall, feeling as if I was risking my life for a madman.

*Oh, wait...I AM!*

"Tayen, you have to stop this, you are going to get us all killed-" I was near tears but my words were wasted. He'd already snuck through the door and into the castle. Aaron and Lanné followed me, behind Tayen.

We exchanged terrified looks then followed Tayen through the hall. He was leading us to The Queen's old room. His eyes getting more excited as he got closer to Omen. I don't know if it was revenge he wanted or Kayleen's safety.

Actually, I knew he wasn't after Kayleen's safety. She was in much more danger now.

"How'd you know the guards were switching right now? How did you set up this perfect timing?" I wondered errantly.

Tayen didn't look at me. He just ran across a corridor to the mouth of the spiral staircase. I took a steadying breath and ran after him.

"Where's Kayleen?" I asked Aaron when he caught up with me.

And finally, someone answered my question.

"The Queen kept her at the wall. She said she had gone as far as she was comfortable with her daughter and she wishes us luck." Tayen spun and faced Aaron.

"She's not The Queen! Omen is The King! Omen defeated her! She gave up! Stop calling her The Queen!" His cold, icy eyes flashed dangerously at Aaron who shrunk back.

Something clicked in my head.

I'd been right. This wasn't Tayen. He wouldn't be cruel to us like he had been. He wouldn't lead us to our death. He wouldn't stand up for Omen. He wouldn't put Kayleen so close to Omen's greedy claws. He wouldn't hurt me so badly.

But I knew who would.

# Chapter 43

"*You're Omen...*" I stared. His scary eyes flickered to me.

"You're crazy. You don't know what you're talking about." He hissed.

"No, I'm not crazy and I know exactly what I'm talking about."

I could see the realization on Aaron and Lanné's faces as they put the pieces together.

"Shut up, you don't have a clue-"

"Yes, I do." I said, stepping up one stair closer, "And you're trying to kill us."

Omen gave in and Tayen's face grinned. "Well, fine. Charade's up. Look who *finally* caught on-"

Then hell broke loose in the middle of the spiral stairs.

Lanné, who was on the stair below us, lunged at him. He kicked her in the jaw. She tumbled backward down the stairs. When she came to a stop near the bottom, she didn't move.

Aaron pulled a stone out of the wall with his mind and threw it at him. Tayen shoved the stone back at Aaron who was too little to hold it and he fell backward too, hitting his head on the wall and then on the rock in his hands as he collapsed on it. His forehead started to bleed.

I ripped my gaze away from Aaron and back to Tayen in time to see him punch me. I staggered to the stair below. Pain and blood exploded from where his knuckles hit my jaw.

I gasped and held my face, watching Tayen move closer. When he was in arms reach, I glared fiercely. I stood up and punched him in the face. Sometimes, I would imagine doing this when he was getting really annoying, but I'd never actually done it.

It felt wrong and it was painful.

His head snapped back from the force of my hit. Shakily, I put my hands on his shoulders and brought my knee up into his stomach making him double over.

I dashed up the stairs, past him. Why I didn't run down the stairs away from him instead of stepping right over him? I don't know.

But sooner than I had expected, Tayen was already up and had grabbed my ankle. He pulled me down and I crashed into the stone steps. He walked toward me, nose bleeding, eyes fiery.

I kicked his left leg out from under him but he caught himself on the wall. I used my bought time to get up and run back down the stairs under his arm.

With a frustrated shout he grabbed the back of my shirt and pulled me back. I gagged and the collar of my shirt ripped.

Tayen pulled out his knife and pinned me against the wall. I grabbed his wrists, and held him off. This time, acidic adrenaline in my veins kept me *just* strong enough to hold him off. But I couldn't last much longer.

I was going to die, I knew it. At the hands of my best friend who was being controlled by my worst enemy.

His eyes were psychotic but I looked deeper.

I looked past Omen's crazy hold on Tayen's body and found him.

There far inside, held back by the **Magic**, was Tayen.

He was watching himself try to kill me and I could see the fear and the tearing pain in his eyes. His real eyes. He had watched everything that Omen had done to us and he was ready to fall to shreds.

I had to let him know that I knew it wasn't really Tayen hurting us.

And I had to know for certain that he knew I loved him. *How!?*

"Omen, I *hate* you -" I gasped, infuriated. Then swore loudly- he faltered momentarily but regained his strength, pushing harder.

The blade quivered just above my

chest- one more second and I-

Then I got an idea.

"He's going to kill me... but Tayen-"

I leaned in close and concentrated on Tayen, far past Omen's control. Then I pressed my lips to his and the knife dropped from his hand. There was a scream from above us and Tayen collapsed. I fell to my knees, surprised.

After a moment of stunned frozenness, he pulled me in and he kissed me again. I heard more tortured screaming that faded into the background as I was overpowered by the feeling of completion. The half of me that had been ripped away all came back at once.

He hugged me close to him and I pulled my face away and hugged him as tight as I could. When I finally looked at his face, his eyes full of indescribable pain but they were alive. And a beautiful, bright, *bright* green.

He was back. My Tayen was back.

*

\*                    \*

Omen **Made** the boy pull out his knife and he tried to stab the girl. She grabbed the boy's arms and pushed back. They struggled for what seemed like years.

Omen watched her face and she glared at him furiously.

"Omen, I *hate* you-" She squeezed her eyes shut and tried to push him away. She yelled a swear and pushed harder.

For a second Omen felt the pain of knowing- she hated him.

Then he was outraged. If he couldn't have her, no one could. Omen pushed against her and watched the knife slowly drop closer to her heart.

He looked at her face. She looked like she was searching for something, she wasn't even looking at Omen anymore. She was looking past him...

*What!?* Omen thought, confused. *How can she-?* Her eyes lit up and she leaned in close and stared through Omen.

"He's going to kill me... but Tayen-"

Then she did the most unexpected thing Omen would have guessed.

She kissed the boy!

As her lips touched the boy's, Omen felt a surge of resistance from the boy and his control snapped. Omen retreated out of the boy's mind and his whole soul burned with excruciating pain, his head pounded and stabbed.

This pain was worse than when he was tortured at night. This pain was a *million* times worse than that.

She had kissed *him*- in the face of death she chose *him*. He choked on his screams and crushed his hands into the stone beneath him.

# Chapter 44

It wasn't until I heard a loud explosion above that I remembered where we were. We both looked up in surprise and terror.

His hands pushed me down the stairs.

"Go! Get out- go, *go*!" He leaned down and pulled Lanné up as he passed her. "I'm sorry, I'm so sorry, it wasn't me-" His voice was cracking in pain as he tried to explain. "Aaron-"

"Believe him for now- Tayen- explain later!" I pushed them down the stairs toward the opening.

We all dashed to the hall and around the corner and sprinted to the main hall. Guards were everywhere.

"Lanné! Aaron!" I called, breaking the momentary freeze.

Aaron started pulling stones out from all around and throwing them at the attacking guards. I noticed a few guards shudder then look around like they were completely lost. Some guards were attacking each other and I knew it was my turn.

I **Sent** myself into and then out of the mind of one of them and grabbed his arm and pulled until I heard a loud pop. I grabbed his helmet and beat my way through the crowd.

I felt the other guard's steel go through my middle but it still had no effect. When most of them were on the ground. I left the guard on the ground, who was still focussed on his dislocated arm, and snapped my eyes open, looking out from the proper eyes.

*

\*   \*

The pain receded and Omen's nightly torture took over. He scrambled to his feet, swaying as he clawed through the pain.

Omen **Entered** the mind of one of his watchmen to see the **Protectors** dashing away from the castle.

He **Amplified** his voice and screamed through the watchmen. He yelled every possible threat and any swear he could think and vowed to kill them, no matter where they ran.

\*

\*                              \*

We dashed across the long front lawn, running as if death was at our heels. It kind of was, I suppose.

We could see The Queen and Kayleen waiting for us at the stone wall.

Flames flew past our heads with hot waves and loud whistles.

"Watch the arrows!" I yelled at the others.

But the arrows stopped and I realized they hadn't even been shooting at us. There were flames in front and all around us- in a small circle.

We were trapped.

I twirled around, desperately searching for a way out. I could find nothing. My eyes landed on Aaron's twisted face. His forehead coated in sweat and a tiny dent in his brow. Hold on, I knew that look.

*He's-*

A giant column of fire rose from our circle and slithered back to the archers at the castle.

"Yeah!" I yelled, punching the air with my fist.

The fire swirled this way and that, burning a complex pattern in the sky. It followed an invisible trail straight to the guards' faces, making them panic and drop their arrows.

While the guards were distracted, Aaron turned back to the wall of flames encircling us and spread the fire apart like a curtain, giving us a clear, straight shot out of the castle grounds.

We split the grass running so fast out of there and only looked back when we heard the piercing, angry, tortured cry of someone who was just so close but lost all it at the last moment.

Omen was screeching his fury after us. His voice most likely amplified by one of his **Spells**. I narrowed my eyes back at the castle, and then gave my jauntiest wave and a grin before disappearing into the dead woods.

# Chapter 45

I almost laughed at the enormity of what just happened. I was still sucking in cool, humid air and my heart was still beating- uncontrollably and painfully fast but still beating nonetheless.

I counted the fact that I was still alive as my life's single most fantastic achievement *ever.*

I was still here, I was still alive, still breathing and still protecting the princess.

I glanced at Tayen- my Tayen, the one I loved not the evil possessed one- he was struggling with himself inside his head.

Then I remembered my kiss. When I was just about to die, the thing I wanted to do in the last few moments of my life was kiss Tayen as hard as I could, just so that he knew I loved him.

Confusion and frustration swept over me. What had I done...

All this amounted to a lot going through a person's mind while they're still sprinting headlong away from their death.

Literally, I had escaped dying by inches. I suddenly almost giggled- absolutely giddy with adrenaline and excitement.

I really had no plan. No idea what the future held. But at least we had a future.

And at that moment, that alone was enough to keep running for.

# Epilogue

That night, after we had run as far as we possibly could have managed, we collapsed, breathing hard on the grass-tucked comfortably into one of the deeper parts of a broad, wild forest.

"Are we far enough away?" Lanné gasped.

"Yeah, I think so." I replied, still choking down air.

"What now?" Aaron asked, quietly.

"I'm not sure." I shook my head. "Let's just focus on living through tonight." I glanced around at everyone's faces. We were all tired and sweaty. *At least we're all able to be tired and sweaty- at least we're all alive...* I thought again, my heart giving a small leap.

"What're we gonna do now?" Kayleen whispered.

"I want you off this island." I decided. "You and your mom."

"We can get off of the island with Fawney." The Queen put in. "He's an old family friend, with a boat. He would most definitely be willing to take us off the island. He was a very close friend of my father's." She took a deep breath.

"You mean Uncle Funny?" Kayleen

said looking up at The Queen. "He always smelled." Kayleen wrinkled her nose.

"Yes, Kayleen, Uncle Funny. He would just be arriving in the next few days." She informed me.

Not seeing any other, safer, available option at present, I agreed. "Fine, it's set, then. We'll go toward the port, keep hidden, and wait for Fawney."

It was silent for a long moment as everyone caught their breath.

Tayen was silent. I looked over at him, he was staring emptily at the ground in front of him.

He was avoiding talking about anything in the past, I could tell.

The fact that he almost watched himself kill us, the way he treated us, what he did... to me...

The sheer guilt and self-loathing

and remorse that was pouring out of his entity made the air around us seem sharp, ready to shatter, impossible to breathe without wincing. His frame was crushed and broken, his face was ashen and dark.

I couldn't tear my eyes from him, but I didn't know what to say.

I didn't know what I wanted to say. I didn't know what I was capable of saying. So I didn't say anything.

Everyone was staring at him now, and feeling their gazes, Tayen attempted his explanation:

"I just- I can't *possibly... begin* to describe what..." His voice cracked and trailed off. He drew in a shaky breath and shook his head again.

"It was Omen. We know he's evil and we know it wasn't you." Lanné appeared beside us and stroked his hair. "It's alright."

He looked up at her, eyes still

hollow- the best thanks he could come up with, though I knew he wouldn't believe her.

"*I* knew it wasn't you, Tayen." Aaron whispered, Tayen turned to look at Aaron. "I *knew* it." Aaron persisted when Tayen didn't respond.

He shuffled closer and hugged Tayen tightly. Tayen slowly and with great strain put his arms around Aaron. Kayleen ran over and jumped in. Tayen quietly stroked her curls and let her hug him.

"You're my big bro," Aaron laughed once Tayen let them go. "The nice kind, too. I know you wouldn't ever actually want to hurt any of us."

Tayen suddenly looked up at me.

His eyes said it all. He knew what Omen had done to me, through him. He figured it was unforgivable.

It was.

I would never forgive Omen for what *he* had done to me, to Tayen and to each one of us.

I narrowed my eyes, analyzing Tayen, watching every infinitesimal move; the play of the breeze in the waves of his hair and the fabric of his clothes, every breath, every tense muscle.

"Calm down already, we still love you." I tried to say it lightly, laugh a little, but my voice shook and my eyes were tearing up even though I was smiling.

Relief melted his body, his taught muscles released and his terrified eyes closed with a silent sigh.

It had not been him who had done all those things. There was nothing to forgive him for. He'd done nothing wrong, yet he'd already suffered more than too much.

"C'mere," I sat up on my knees, grabbed him and pulled him close, he wrapped his arms around me and held me tightly.

"You have no idea..." he whispered in my ear after a moment. It was so quiet, I wasn't sure whether the others could hear what he was saying or not. "I wanted to... kill myself. I wanted to die."

I shook my head wildly and put my head on his shoulder. "Shut up, okay? Just forget about it. It's done." I mumbled softly, somehow soothingly.

I hadn't realized just how much I actually loved him and needed him- as a right-hand-man, as a battle partner, as a best friend, as everything- until he was gone.

It seemed like eons before one of us moved to pull away and suddenly it felt as though we'd only held each other for a split second.

I finally looked past him at the others, trying to move on from that massive wave of emotion, I returned my focus to

Kayleen and the rest of my family. Keeping them safe.

"Well, we'd better get to started if we're going to set this plan in action before Omen gets his men after us." I said, but taking in all the weary faces, I added, "...But first, sleep."

"Ah! Thank youuu..." Aaron grinned and collapsed on his back.

Lanné let out a long breath and smiled. "Sounds like a plan, Stan." She saluted, then curled up on the ground.

No one else spoke and one by one, we all slipped away into dreams-

Except me.

I couldn't sleep, even though my body was dead freaking tired- and killing me, by the way. I was sore all over. *Hm... Wonder why?* I thought, rubbing my jaw where I was sure a nasty bruise would turn up sooner or later.

But I had too many buzzing questions swirling in my brain to pay too much attention to that.

*How will we protect Kayleen if she's away from us? Who could go with them? Can I really trust this Fawney? How will we possibly fight Omen by ourselves?*

*And Tayen...*

I looked over at his sleeping face, I knew he still wouldn't fully forgive himself for a long time even though, clearly, nothing he had done these past three days was his fault.

*Should I tell him why I kissed him? Should I even mention it?*

*I should probably leave him alone for a while. I should. Let him calm down.*

*But what if he thinks I don't* want *to talk about it...*

In my frustration I realized I'd

yanked two fistfuls of grass out of the ground, leaving angry bald spots in the forest floor.

I threw the grass away with as much fury as one can possibly portray when chucking grass at trees. Then, in the quiet moment in my head, my eyes fell back to Tayen's face.

As I watched him, he winced silently in his sleep. I wondered what he was dreaming about.

I shook my head and rubbed my eyes. *Why can't life just be easy? Because then it wouldn't be fun?*

*Yeah, so far it's been oodles of fun...*

I rolled my eyes and tried not to think about the unclear future. I just focused on survival. I had to make all the right moves.

Because after all, any wrong move could be our last, right?

The Protectors: Once Upon a Catastrophe

# The Protectors: Once Upon a Catastrophe

## Acknowledgements

There's so many people I want to thank for helping me make this little dream of mine come true, I always wanted to be a published author and I'd be lying if I claimed that I did it all by myself.

First, I just want to give thanks to God, who gave me everything. He knew about my passion for writing before anyone else. He blessed me incredibly with so many good people and gifts. He gave me every opportunity, every word, the desire and the education and the capacity to imagine, create and dream.

To Mum, Dad and Rachel, for putting up with me as I spent endless hours writing. My family believed that I could achieve anything I put my mind and heart into, they listened, read and learned along with me the whole way.

To all my friends, who were always willing to read, suggest things and gush about my book. Thank you Caitlyn, Jamie, Christie, Josh, Joel, Eli, Sarah, Jenny, Erin, Moira and everyone else who listened to me talk about publishing my book and didn't call me crazy.

To my teachers, Mrs. Ricioppo, Mrs. King, Mrs. Whittal-Williams, who taught, encouraged, supported and believed.

To my Drama 20-30 class, for being the audience of my first public reading.

To everyone who offered advice and help with

*publishing, marketing, distributing, etc. Thank you, my book would be on a shelf gathering dust without your guidance.*

*To the bands and artists I listened to when I needed inspiration. My Chemical Romance, Paramore, Marianas Trench, Metric, Death Cab For Cutie, Chiodos, LIGHTS, Pierce the Veil, and more. Thanks for stirring up the creativity and emotion in me when I couldn't or didn't want to.*

*To J. K. Rowling, because her "Harry Potter" series was the first series I ever read, and because of it, I immediately fell in love with stories and characters and other worlds. I was introduced to the magic of fiction and assured that it's okay to always have my nose in a book. And to James Patterson, who's novel "Maximum Ride: The Angel Experiment" gave me the inspirational kick I needed, something to look up to and something to aspire toward.*

*To all the people that helped me learn what it really feels like to be loved, to love, to be encouraged, to be disposed of, to defend, to be defended, to mend, to be mended, to be strong, to be afraid, to trust and to be betrayed, to be accepted, to be rejected, to protect and to be protected.*

*Without feeling these things, I wouldn't have been able to put people into my characters, or life into my story.*

*To all those who have read, are reading or will read my stories- and to you, reader, thank you- you have good taste in books. ;)*

# The Protectors: Once Upon a Catastrophe

# The Protectors: Once Upon a Catastrophe

Watch for

# The Protectors

## Part 2: Life on Karma's Blacklist

# The Protectors: Once Upon a Catastrophe

# Prologue

After everything we'd been through you'd think that simply waiting would be a little easier to take than, say, near-death brushes and murderous phychos and assassins. Well, no, not really, not for me. It's agonizingly frustrating. I wasn't gifted with patience.

Think about it. Waiting; there's nothing to do and there's nothing you *can* do to make anything go faster. The more I meditate on this, the crazier it makes me.

So never mind, don't think about it.

Here's the funny part, though; when something *does* happen to break the boredom spell, there's nothing I wouldn't give to make it go away- well, something like *this*, I mean...

I pressed myself tighter against the tree, focussed on keeping my breathing even and silent, Kayleen shook against me as I strained my ears to hear the sound of approaching footsteps.

The policy right now, if we were to be spotted by *anyone* throughout the kingdom is, "shoot first, ask questions later". I don't appreciate it all that much, to say the least.

It isn't as though we are, or have any intentions of, harming anyone- well, except the *king* and his cronies, so I guess I just lied.

I hope you heard me say "king" with distain and sarcastic disgust, because that's how I meant it. The way I see it, if a person steals a crown, that doesn't make them a monarch, it makes them a theif and a murderer.

But that argument's not gonna do me much good if people will sooner listen to the tyrant than the truth.

A loud thump jolted me- it wasn't really all that loud, but I'd been listening intently in the quiet for so long, the sudden noise registered in my brain as a colossal crash.

In reality, Lanné had dropped from the tree branch she had been perched on and landed in front of the stranger. Surprised, the stranger fell backward with a cry. After a brief, silent pause, the stranger jolted again.

"Where am I? Who are you- I don't *know* anything!" The person, the man, sounded terrified. He had a gravelly voice-rough, as though many, many years of use had worn it out, either that or he smoked a pipe. Whichever it was, he sounded as though he wasn't in the best shape, and we'd scared the living daylights out of him. "I- I can't move my legs-!" He shouted suddenly.

"Tayen!" Lanné hissed. I heard dead leaves rustle violently as the man was set free suddenly and he scrambled to his feet.

"You were out on a walk and you saw a bear- it spooked you and you don't want anyone else to stumble across it." Lanné told him. "Warn others not to go into the forest-"

"What are you talking about- get away from me, witch!" The man had been backing away from the small, thin, spooky girl in front of him, now he broke into a run, breathlessly trying to escape her.

I slid out from between the tree and Kayleen and spoke urgently. "You took too long to *tell* him what to remember, he was already developing memories- we gotta do it again or he'll bust us-"

"You get him back here then, we cant risk going too far from here, we'll be too close to the city-" Lanné told me while The Queen appeared from where she was hidden and took her daughter, Kayleen, into her arms, trying to get her to calm.

Aaron dropped from a tree limb and Tayen appeared behind me. "Well, hurry up! Don't just stand around, talkin'." Aaron told Lanné and I.

I shut my eyes and sensed the man's scattered mind as he moved in a hap-hazard pattern, away from us.

I **Saw** the forest, tumbling past as the man ran, tripping and turning and losing his way. I felt cold dread in his mind, terror- he was horrified at the thought of being lost, he thought we were going to find him and kill him.

If I could've rolled my eyes at this

point, I would've before I stepped out into the open- moving outside the confines of this poor man's mind.

He was maybe in his late fifties, and rail-thin. A tangle of long salt-and-pepper hair made up most of his body mass, I was sure.

I was a ghost, an invisible spirit, to him in this state. I knew this was probably going to scare him even more senseless, but what other choice did I have? I pressed my hands against his shoulders and pushed hard, trying to get him to stop running. He cried out and panicked, twisting away.

He swept his arms widely around him, feeling for what pushed him. I watched as he began to wheeze loudly, and faster than he had been. He pulled his arms in again, fists clentched, shaking. Fear resonated in his wild gaze, then his pupils dialated even further, to the size of small plates, before his muscles gave out- his arms dropped and he tippedforeward, collapsing in the dirt and leaves.

I let out a long breath in frustration.

I returned to my body, keeping my eyes shut tight, braced for the splitting headache that attacked me every time I used my power, like clockwork.

Once the worst had passed, I pulled myself off the ground, brushing junk off my jeans. "C'mon. He's out cold." I gestured for Tayen to follow me, still squinting from the throbbing in my brain.

I led him to where the man lay, still unconscious.

"How hard did you hit him?" Tayen asked, head tilted slightly as we stared at him.

"I didn't." I insisted, Tayen gave me a very small sideways smile before he turned his eyes back to the poor unconscious man.

With a little supernatural help from Tayen, the man- still out like a light- got to his feet and clumsily shuffled along behind us as we walked back again, deeper into the heart of the forest.

Luckily the man hadn't run too far away from us, and it didn't take long to get back to the others.

When the man came to, Lanné played with his memory a bit- told him about the alleged bear attack- and sent him on his way. He took off, running away from us once again scared as all get out.

*Rough day for that guy.* I thought, as his shadow disappeared through the branches.

The sky had turned silver, I realized, as the heavy atmosphere of empty seconds passing, seemingly endless waiting, threatened to drift back down over me. Just as I turned to Tayen to say, "I can't take this anymore," Aaron made a sound from his perch up in a tree. He had our small, brass telescope pressed to his right eye.

"Guys-" He repeated after no one

had responded the first time.

"What?" Tayen called back up.

"What's Fawney's boat look like again?"

"Small, very small," The Queen reminded him, "You should see him at the helm, he's a big man with a beard-"

"I think I see him! He just crossin' the bay!" Aaron told us excitedly.

"Well, let's get to the docks- we're about a day away on foot, let's move!" I said, as Aaron climbed down, the kid resembling a monkey a little too much.

I moved at a brisk pace, I was anxious, but incredibly relieved to finally be through with the waiting. I was ready to move again, to run, fight, negotiate, feel adrenaline in my system... I was ready to get back into the game.

Chances are slim that I'd relish this excitement for long, but I'd savour it while it lasted. Because sooner than later, I was sure I'd be reintroduced to all the fear, the anxiety, the doubt, the uncertainty, the danger and I'd hate it.

Sooner than later, I'd be reminded that this is no game; this is my job, this is my life as a protector... But I love it.

The Protectors: Once Upon a Catastrophe

REBECCA BOURQUE was fourteen when
she started writing THE PROTECTORS, her
first book series.
Inspired by the magic and adventures of other
amazing authors and their characters from a
very young age, she dreamed that someday she
might tell tales that other people could escape
into and fall in love with.
At eighteen, she would proudly tell you that
she achieved one of her most precious
aspirations, and she plans to write more stories,
for as long as she believes in magic and
adventure.